Baseball

A TICKET TO THE BIGS

BY

RAYMOND BEAN

www.raymondbean.com

Raymond Bean books

Baseball: A Ticket to the Bigs

<u>Sweet Farts Series</u>
Sweet Farts #1
Sweet Farts #2 Rippin' It Old School
Sweet Farts #3 Blown Away

<u>School Is A Nightmare Series</u>
School Is A Nightmare #1
First Week, Worst Week
School Is A Nightmare #2 The Field Trip
School Is A Nightmare #3 Shocktober
School Is A Nightmare #4
Yuck Mouth and the Thanksgiving Miracle
School Is A Nightmare – Quadzilla
(Books 1-4) Special Edition
School Is A Nightmare #5
Winter Breakdown (Coming Fall 2013)
School Is A Nightmare #6 Cupid's Crush
(Coming Winter 2014)

For Stacy, Ethan, and Chloe

Interested in scheduling an
author visit or web based author talk?
Email us at raymondbeanbooks@gmail.com

Contents

1. Visit The Clouds — 1

2. Will's One Thing — 4

3. Multiheaded Monster — 8

4. You're A Poser — 12

5. That's What I
   Thought You'd Say — 16

6. That's Cute — 19

7. The Tunnel — 22

8. It Makes Yankee Stadium Look Like
   A Booger — 30

9. baseballhound.com — 39

10. This Isn't Disneyland — 41

11. Full-Court
    Press Conference — 47

12. Post-Press Conference — 54

13. The Clear
    Coffee Company — 55

14. I Already Do — 59

15. Sports Blogger — 69

16. The Deal — 71

17. The Scrap Heap — 76

18.	Wiffle Balls	89
19.	T-Bone Stake	93
20.	The Pitching Left Fielder	96
21.	You're Still A Loser	99
22.	T-Rex And Goggles	102
23.	The Sleepy Catcher	108
24.	More Gum On The Jersey	110
25.	Ripturd	114
26.	Edges	117
27.	Get On The Field	125
28.	The Guys In The Booth	131
29.	Buzz	143
30.	Walk-Off Home Run	146
31.	They Think You're A Lunatic	153
32.	Treemendous	164
33.	No One Was Electrocuted	169
34.	Charlie And The Chocolate Bar	173
35.	The Leather Card	178
36.	Frenzy	182

37.	Fingers Crossed	186
38.	The Package	187
39.	W-43-I-52-LL-543-IZ-5954-DA-591-M-797-AN	194
40.	The Kid Can't Play	199
41.	Welcome To The Circus	201
42.	You're So Money	204
43.	Oh Boy	209
44.	I'm Chopping Onions	216
45.	The Ten-Year Old Starter	220
46.	Batter Up	226
47.	How Good He Used To Be	230
48.	You're A Star	232
49.	Bad Idea	235
50.	Used To Be	238
51.	The Talk	241
52.	Statisticationer	244
53.	Operation Power Tunnel	248
54.	It's Gone	251
55.	People Will Think You're Nuts	257
56.	Power Shift	264

1

VISIT THE CLOUDS

When Major League Baseball announced that it was adding the Long Island Riptide to the league, fans all over the country buzzed with excitement. Most people thought it was a mistake, because New York had always been the home of the Yankees and the Mets. Building a fan base wouldn't be easy for a new team. The owner, Will Panzell, added to the pressure by promising fans a brand-new stadium, the best players from around the world, and a personal guarantee to bring home a World Series championship in two years or less!

Will's dad was the famous billionaire Lawrence Panzell. Lawrence had made his fortune in the stock market. Everything he touched during his lifetime turned to gold. Will was not blessed with his father's golden touch.

Lawrence always used to tell Will, "You walk through life with your head in the clouds. It's nice to visit the clouds, but you mustn't *live* in them, son." Will always nodded his head and pretended to understand what his dad meant, but he really had no idea what his father was talking about.

Lawrence worried about his son's tendency to give up. Will started several different companies while in his twenties, attempted to make several "brilliant" inventions during his thirties, and once even went searching for lost treasure for three years in the jungles of South America. All Will's attempts ended in the same way: if he didn't fail, he quit. Lawrence never stopped believing in his son, but secretly he worried that Will would never find his true calling in life. Before he died, Lawrence's last words to his son were, "Pick one thing—not your nose—and be great at it, my boy."

2

WILL'S ONE THING

Upon his father's death, Will inherited a huge sum of money. The "one thing" he chose to be great at was being the owner of a professional baseball team. He didn't know much about baseball, but a Yankees game was on TV in the hospital room when his father passed. Will saw it as a sign.

His father had always been a huge baseball fan. When alive, he'd mentioned to Will loads of times that he would have loved to own a team but never felt he had the time to do it right.

Within months of his father's death, Will started construction on the Lawrence Panzell Memorial Stadium on the eastern end of Long Island, New York. He didn't have a team or the approval from Major League Baseball, but that didn't stop him. His accountant told him he was crazy, his mother told him she didn't approve, and his lawyers said it would never work. Will ignored them all.

When Will and his lawyers finally approached MLB with the idea for an expansion team, the league didn't want a new team. Will remained very determined, and after a few months of meetings they believed in him. It didn't hurt that he had billions of dollars to invest. His lawyers drew up the longest contract Will had ever seen. After he signed it, he became the owner and general manager of the newest team in baseball, the Long Island Riptide.

The winter before the first season, Will remained extremely secretive about the details of the team. Even the commissioner of baseball didn't know anything beyond the fact that the team would be called the Riptide.

Construction crews worked around the clock in order to finish the stadium in time for opening day on April 7. No one but the crew and Will's lawyers was allowed inside the stadium at any time. Construction workers had to sign contracts agreeing not to leak a word of the stadium to anyone. Never before had a stadium been built with so much secrecy.

Rumors about the team swirled on sports websites, ESPN, and New York sports radio stations. They all had a field day trying to predict which players would end up on the team. One rumor said Will planned to bring the best players from Japan, South America, and the Caribbean to play for the Riptide. Another reported he had already struck secret deals with some of baseball's best players, and that they would all break their current contracts days before spring training in February.

Will's favorite rumor was one he started himself. He called in to one of the sports radio morning shows. He used a fake name and claimed to be a worker at a robotics company, then told the hosts that Will Panzell had placed an order for fourteen robots that looked human but had the ability to play baseball. He even faxed the show a fake order form. The show's hosts talked about the possibility of a cyborg baseball team coming to New York. The story even made the papers for a few days—until someone did a little research and realized that the robot company listed on the order form didn't exist.

Will remained pleased with his prank. After all, the story garnered tons of attention in the papers and got people talking about the team. What more could a manager ask for?

3

MULTIHEADED MONSTER

Tommy Spence was the only kid in fourth grade with a Long Island Riptide jersey.

"That team is for losers," someone said from the back of the bus. Silence fell over the bus, which was usually loud and chaotic. Everyone could sense that trouble was brewing—and kids like to watch trouble unfold.

Tommy dropped his backpack onto the seat directly behind the bus driver. "I think they're pretty cool," he said, straining to see who was talking to him.

Chris, who had the eyes of a snake and the soul of a rat, smirked. "Only a loser would wear a Riptide jersey," he said. "They're not even a real team."

"They're the first new team to join Major League Baseball since the Diamondbacks and the Devil Rays in 1998," Tommy said defensively. He expected someone to agree with him. No one did.

"The Devil Rays aren't called the Devil Rays anymore. They're just the Rays," Chris said. "Get your facts straight." Kids on both sides of the aisle laughed.

Tommy felt the warm rush of embarrassment wash over him. "You know what I mean," he tried. "There hasn't been an expansion team in a long time. I think it's pretty cool."

"That makes one of you," Eddie, who was the second-nastiest kid on the bus, said. Kids laughed more. It was the worst kind of laughter, too, the kind that only seems to exist when adults aren't watching.

A boy in the middle of the bus, whose name Tommy didn't know, knelt on his seat. "I bet you can't name one player on the Riptide," he challenged, loud enough for the entire bus to hear.

"I can't," Tommy said. "No one can, because they haven't announced their players yet." Silence fell over the bus.

"Exactly!" the kid shouted. Tommy felt like he was on trial and a team of obnoxious child lawyers was questioning him. "Can you believe him? How can he root for a team if he doesn't even know who the players are?" the kid added.

The silence deepened. Tommy was no stranger to being teased by the "cool" kids. He always wondered why no one ever stuck up for him. There had to be other kids on the bus that felt sorry for him, but none of them ever said anything.

"It doesn't matter to me. I like that we'll have a new team to root for. I might even get season tickets."

"Then you're a loser," Chris declared from the back, making an *L* on his forehead with his hand.

The bus felt like a multiheaded monster to Tommy, and all the heads were heckling him at the same time. Kids like Chris, Eddie, and what's-his-face in the middle of the bus ruled with an iron fist. They lived to insult, and they were good at it. Tommy was no match for their cruelty.

He had told on kids a few times over the years, but the bus drivers never did anything that stopped it for long. Most drivers grunted, yelled, or gave some useless advice like, "Just tell them you don't like it."

Right, Tommy always thought. *I'm going to tell Chris and his miserable band of half-wits that I don't "like it" when they tease me. What a joke.*

4

YOU'RE A POSER

Tommy loved to collect baseball jerseys. His parents always bought him new ones for special occasions like birthdays and Christmas. His grandparents usually got him one for good report cards, Thanksgiving, Valentine's Day, and just about any other excuse they could think of to buy him something. Tommy was their one and only grandchild and they treated him like royalty.

He had jerseys from almost every team, and several from local teams like the Mets and the

Yankees. His favorites were old-time jerseys with names like Mantle, Robinson, and Ruth. He loved baseball trivia and knew more about the game than most adults.

His dad always warned him about wearing jerseys of New York rivals—like the Red Sox—to school, but Tommy wore them anyway.

The Red Sox were the toughest team to wear. One time when he was at the mall with his dad, an adult said, "When you get home, you should burn that shirt in your yard, kid." Tommy faked an uncomfortable smile. "I'm not kiddin'," the man said seriously. "That rag needs to get burned!"

"I tried to warn you," his dad said at the time.

Tommy blogged about the incident on his baseball website. When he started the blog, he handed out flyers at school, hoping other kids would follow it. Most kids crumpled up his flyers and threw them away. A bunch ended up on the floor of the classroom. On the bus, kids made them into paper airplanes and threw them across the bus. His blog, baseballhound. com, had four followers; he was pretty sure they were his parents and his grandparents. He tried to write a post a day, and some days he put up two or more. They were usually short pieces on a player or something that had happened in a game that day.

Tommy secretly hoped he'd be discovered by *Sports Illustrated* or ESPN and become a sportswriter. He made the mistake of telling Jimmy DeChamps one day at indoor recess. Jimmy told everyone that Tommy thought he was a great sportswriter. Andrew, the meanest kid in Tommy's class, said, "You're a poser. Sportswriters aren't weirdos like you; they're cool. I bet they're nothing like you, because you're a poser. You walk around in baseball stuff every day, and you stink at baseball. That makes you a poser," Andrew said.

"Actually, many sportswriters are guys like me who just happen to have a love of sports," Tommy said.

"Who told you that?"

"My grandma. And she's right: I know from reading their articles. Many famous sportswriters and analysts were never athletes themselves, but simply fans of the game," Tommy said, smiling.

His grandfather told him to smile when he talked to people because it increased the chances of them liking you. Even though he always tried, it didn't seem to work for Tommy. Kids didn't like him much.

5

THAT'S WHAT I THOUGHT YOU'D SAY

The first member of the team Will shared with the media was its manager, Morgan St. John. He announced it on ESPN in November, well before the first season.

Morgan was a former all-star and one of Will's father's favorite players of all time. Will knew he'd be the perfect guy for the job. Morgan was the assistant manager for a team in Japan when Will called and offered him the job.

"I'm flattered by the offer, Mr. Panzell," he said. "I've always dreamed of being a manager in the big leagues. It's amazing that you've convinced MLB to let you start a new team."

"You'll come to learn that I'm a very smart man, Morgan. I'm not bragging, but you'll get to know my true genius if you choose to take the job. You'll also be managing some of the most talented players in baseball today. I'm basically offering you the best job in the whole world. If you don't take it, you're completely nuts."

"It sounds like you have quite a team planned. I'd love to learn more. The excitement about the Riptide has made it all the way over here. People in Japan are really excited about it. Who are your players?"

"I can't share any names, Morgan, but I can promise you'll be managing an all-star-level team. For now, all I'll say is that it's probably the best team in the history of baseball. If you want the opportunity, you'll just have to trust me. If you aren't interested, though, I'm sure I'll find someone for the job."

Morgan didn't hesitate. He knew this was his chance to manage in the big leagues, and an opportunity like it might not come along again.

"I'll be on the next plane to New York. I can't wait to get started," he said.

"That's what I thought you'd say," Will said. "There's no rush. Just get here by February first and prepare for greatness."

6

THAT'S CUTE

Morgan arrived in New York on February 1 as agreed. He couldn't wait to spend the next few months planning his practices, thinking about how to beat other teams, and meeting his players.

The day he arrived, he talked to Will on the phone and asked for the roster once more.

"The roster is completely confidential, and it's too risky to tell anyone," Will said.

"It's pretty strange preparing for a season and not knowing who my players will be," Morgan tried.

"They'll be awesome!" Will said enthusiastically. "Just imagine the most awesome players you can think of and plan for them. Why don't you practice on the Xbox or something?"

"I can't practice on a video game," Morgan argued.

"I have to go, Morgan. If I were you, I'd use the Xbox. It's a fine research tool. Remember what I told you when we first talked: You've got to trust me. Have I ever steered you wrong before?" Will asked.

"We've never met," Morgan reminded him.

"Well then, you have no reason to doubt me. We'll meet soon enough. I'm holding a press conference on February fifteenth to announce the players. I want you there with me. Are you free?"

"Of course. I'll meet you right now if you like. I'm dying to know who's on this team."

"That's cute, Morgan. We'll talk soon," Will said, and hung up.

7

THE TUNNEL

The day of the press conference, Will sent a car to pick Morgan up from his motel. Ron, the driver, was a short man with a thick, black, Rollie Fingers mustache. It was curled up on both ends and looked like it took a lot of effort and time to create. Morgan tried asking him questions about the team and about Will. Ron wasn't playing along.

"What's it like to work for Mr. Panzell?" Morgan asked.

"I'm not supposed to talk about that," Ron replied.

"Can you tell me a little about the stadium? I hear it's amazing."

"Can't talk about that, either."

"What can you talk about?"

"Nothing to do with Mr. Panzell or the team. You may, however, ask me about my mustache." His mustache was impressive, and Morgan had several questions—like *How do you make it curl?* He decided to avoid the temptation and stayed on topic instead.

"No thanks. It's fascinating, but I'll save those questions for another time."

Ron drove, and they were silent for a while. Country music played on the radio. Ron hummed along twirling his moustache with his free hand. There'd been traffic near his motel, but the roads became less crowded the farther they traveled. Eventually the roads emptied and in the distance, Morgan could see the stadium coming into view. Even from a distance and through a car window, it looked impressive. He'd played in loads of stadiums around the world, but this one was unique. The outer sides of the stadium were designed to resemble waves, so it looked like a massive tidal wave soaring above the trees. Morgan felt butterflies in his stomach. The last time he'd felt them was his first day as a pro player, over fifty years before. His mom always told him that butterflies in his stomach were a sign that something special was about to happen. Seeing the Riptide stadium for the first time caused those old memories to come flooding back.

Without warning, Ron turned the car down a narrow dirt road. Morgan lost his balance and almost spilled his coffee.

"Shortcut?" Morgan asked.

"You could say that," Ron replied.

The car rattled along the dirt road, kicking up dust. On both sides of the road, farms stretched as far as Morgan could see. Several windmills spun in the breeze. Morgan wasn't familiar with Long Island, but it was clear the stadium was built extremely far from New York City. The smell of cabbage was thick in the air.

"The stadium is really far out here," Morgan stated.

"Yep," Ron replied. The car turned down another dirt road, this one even narrower than the one before. An old barn sat at the end of the road. Ron clicked a button on the dashboard and the large red door of the barn opened.

"You might want to slow down, Ron," Morgan warned.

"No need," Ron stated.

Morgan braced for impact. They raced into the barn and Morgan thought they'd crash right into the back wall, but before he knew it, the car rolled down a slight hill and into a paved tunnel that ran under the barn. Ron clicked the button again to close the barn door behind them.

"What is this?" Morgan asked.

"It's a tunnel, sir."

"I can see that. Why is it here?"

"Can't tell you that, sir. We're almost there, though. Sit back and relax."

They drove through the tunnel for several minutes. Morgan noticed massive fans mounted on the ceiling. They were hung every twenty feet or so and were absolutely huge.

"What's the deal with the fans?" Morgan asked.

"Sir, at what point are you going to realize that I won't be answering your questions? I suggest you sit back and relax. We'll be there any second now."

A few minutes later they pulled into a giant, round, underground room. Morgan thought it might be a parking lot, but there weren't parking lines or any other cars parked in it.

Ron parked and Morgan got out. He looked up at the soaring ceiling, which was easily a hundred feet high. Hanging from the ceiling about ten feet above his head was the largest fan he'd ever seen. It must have been ninety feet tall and had gigantic metal blades. Morgan almost asked

Ron what it was for, but knew he wouldn't get an answer.

Ron didn't get out of the car, but he rolled down the window and handed Morgan a rubber mask. "You're going to have to put this on."

"Are you kidding?" Morgan asked.

"In case you haven't noticed, I don't kid much," Ron said. "Mr. Panzell's orders."

"I don't get it. Is this a joke?"

"Afraid not. Mr. Panzell won't have it any other way."

Morgan held the mask out to get a better look. It was orange and had green hair. "This looks like an Oompa-Loompa mask," Morgan said.

"That's because it is an Oompa-Loompa mask, sir," Ron said.

Morgan considered his situation for a moment. He wanted to be a big-league manager, but so far the whole experience seemed completely bizarre.

"May I ask why he wants me to wear an Oompa-Loompa mask?"

"You may not," Ron said, twisting his mustache some more.

"You haven't answered one question this whole time and I was fine with it, but if you want me to put on this mask, you're going to have to tell me why."

"You're probably better off not asking so many questions, Mr. St. John."

"I need an answer to this one, Ron. I'm a grown man, for goodness' sake. Why am I putting on this mask?"

"You haven't met Mr. Panzell yet, have you, sir?"

"Nope."

"It'll make more sense once you meet him. Take my word for it. Let's just say he's not as serious as I am."

"You mean to tell me that he wants me to put on this mask for his entertainment?"

"Yep, that's what I'm telling you."

"And if I don't put it on?"

"I can drive you back to the motel."

"All right. I've come all the way from Japan for this opportunity. I guess I'll play along," Morgan said, pulling the rubber mask over his face.

8

IT MAKES YANKEE STADIUM LOOK LIKE A BOOGER

Morgan hadn't worn a rubber mask since he was a kid. He immediately remembered how much he hated wearing them. It made his face hot, and the sound of his breath inside the mask was magnified enough to make him claustrophobic. The eye slots were so narrow he was only able to make out glimpses of light.

"Excellent," Ron said. "Mr. Panzell will be very pleased."

Ron got out of the car and led him to an elevator. They went up a few floors, walked down a hallway, and then entered an office. Even with the mask on, Morgan could tell that the office was dark. He could hear the sound of a video game in the room.

"Good luck, Mr. St. John. I'll see you around," Ron said, leaving the room and closing the door. Morgan stood where he was, feeling confused and a little embarrassed.

"Morgan St. John, in the living flesh," someone said from the other side of the room.

"Mr. Panzell?" Morgan asked.

"The one and only. You wore the mask! I love it!" he said, snapping a picture. "Go on and take it off. You look ridiculous."

"Thank you. What's the deal with the mask, anyway? Ron wouldn't tell me anything."

"I was testing you. A lot of people wouldn't have agreed to wear it. It shows you're a team player. You didn't know why I wanted you to wear it, but you trusted me. That means a lot."

"Wasn't quitting my job and moving here from Japan without meeting you enough to prove my trust?"

"You got me. I forgot about that part. Yeah, I guess that should have been enough. Oh well. It was fun anyway!"

Morgan had expected a polished business-man in a fancy suit with a team of serious-looking lawyers and assistants following him around. Instead, Will wore a Riptide jersey and faded SpongeBob SquarePants bathing shorts. The wet bathing suit dripped on the rug beneath him. He also wore black socks pulled up to his knees and those Adidas sports slippers athletes and prisoners are fond of wearing. Since Will was neither athlete nor prisoner, the slippers looked particularly odd on him.

"Mr. Panzell?" Morgan asked, confused.

"That's my name, Coach," Will said, tossing a video game controller onto his large desk. "Don't wear it out."

Morgan leaned in to shake Will's hand but was instead engulfed in an extremely tight hug. Will's wet bathing suit got the front of Morgan's pants wet.

"I know you're happy to see me, Morgan, but you didn't have to wet your pants," Will said, laughing at his own joke.

"I didn't. It was because of your wet bathing suit."

"You don't have to be embarrassed that you wet your front porch, Morgan. It happens to the best of us. I've had accidents loads of times. It happened to me one time on an airplane. Very embarrassing!"

"I didn't wet my pants," Morgan said, annoyed.

"If you say so," Will said, winking. "I'm not judging. Let's agree to disagree."

Morgan wasn't sure what to do or say next. It was hard for him to tell whether Will was kidding, crazy, or both.

Will sat back down in his desk chair and resumed his video game, which had been on pause since Morgan took off the mask.

"I still don't get why I had to wear a mask."

"I told you. I was checking to see if you were a team player. You played along. You passed."

"That's the only reason?"

"Yep…and because I love masks. Don't you?"

"Not particularly."

"Too bad. I'm working on our mascot. Come have a look and let me know what you think," he said, pausing his game again and tossing the controller onto his desk. He motioned for Morgan to follow him over to the couch.

The office was massive. It looked more like an apartment than an office. The far wall by the couches was glass from floor to ceiling. Costumes were laid out on the couch. Morgan walked past them and over to the windows. He looked out on center field. It was the most beautiful stadium Morgan had ever seen. It was so breathtaking, he teared up a little.

"Are you crying, Mr. St. John?" Will asked sarcastically.

"Nope. Just something in my eye," Morgan lied. "It is impressive. Very impressive."

"It's *the* best stadium in the world. Makes Yankee Stadium look like a booger."

"I don't know about that, but it's certainly a thing of beauty."

"You have no idea. This place is like no other stadium ever built." Will joined Morgan at the window, slinging his arm around Morgan's shoulders. "Take it in, Morgo. This is where we're going to win a world championship."

"One step at a time, boss. We don't even have a team yet."

"Oh, I've got that all taken care of. Don't you worry your pretty orange head about it," he said.

Morgan continued to admire the new stadium. Will walked back to his desk and resumed his video game.

"Don't we have a press conference to get to?" Morgan asked when he realized Will had sat back down.

Will paused the game again. "You're right! I knew I was forgetting something. I'm very easily distracted. This is why *you're* the manager. Yes, we have a stinkin' press conference. Let's do this!" He led Morgan out of the office.

"Mr. Panzell, do you think we should chat a bit about the team before we meet with the press?" Morgan said, trying to keep up with Will.

"Nope."

"If I'm asked questions about the team, I won't be able to answer any of them."

"Exactly. I'll do all the talking. You just follow my lead."

"If you say so. Um…Mr. Panzell, are you going to change before the conference?"

"What you see is what you get. I just came from swimming, and I don't feel like changing."

"Do you swim on a team?" Morgan asked.

Will did not swim on a team, but knowing that Morgan thought he could be a competitive swimmer made him smile.

"No, but I'm flattered that you would think I'm a professional swimmer," Will said. "I built a gigantic pool in the basement for the players. I figured it would be a great opportunity for me to finally learn to swim. I take lessons every Tuesday and Thursday with Miss Kathy."

Morgan couldn't tell whether Will was kidding or not, but from the look on his face, he was being serious. "Good for you, Mr. Panzell. It's never too late to learn something new."

"I can probably get you into the class if you need lessons."

"That's very generous, sir, but fortunately I already know how to swim."

"Lucky!" Will said. The way he said it reminded Morgan of a child.

"Should we head to that press conference now, boss?"

"Yes, indeed. Are you ready?" Will asked.

"As ready as I can be, I guess."

"Great! Let's go! I'll let you do all the talking," he said, winking.

A giant gumball machine stood in the hall-way. Will turned it several times, releasing a few gumballs, and popped them into his mouth.

"Help yourself," Will instructed. "It doesn't even cost any money. We have a little time. Let's take a tour of my masterpiece."

Morgan tried to hold back his smile as he walked behind Will, but couldn't. The combination of the jersey, the dripping bathing suit, and the slippers and black socks was just too much. Their phone conversations had given Morgan a feeling that Will was a strange guy, but meeting him in person confirmed it.

9

BASEBALLHOUND.COM

Tommy was home watching ESPN and waiting for the press conference with Riptide owner Will Panzell. He blogged as he watched.

February 15

I can't wait to see who will play for the Riptide. The manager, Morgan St. John, and the owner and general manager, Will Panzell, will give a press conference today. I'm hopeful they'll finally reveal their roster. I've been waiting all winter.

I did a little research on Morgan St. John. He was a very talented player in the early sixties. He played for the Giants, the Cubs, and the Tigers. Morgan was assistant managing in Japan for the past few seasons. He's also been a pitching coach in Venezuela, a batting coach in Mexico, and a first base coach in the Caribbean. He should be a great coach for the Riptide. I'll post more after the press conference.

—Tommy

10

THIS ISN'T DISNEYLAND

Will opened a door that led to the Riptide's dugout.

Morgan had been in a load of dugouts in his day, but this was by far the nicest. It felt more like a luxury suite than a dugout. The bench was basically a long, raised, leather couch. TV screens lined the walls. Candy dispensers, drink coolers, and snacks were set up all over. A director's chair—like the ones on movie sets—sat in one corner. COACH ST. JOHN was printed on the back.

"What do you think?" Will asked, patting the chair so Morgan would sit down.

"I don't know what to say. It's almost too nice," he said, sitting in the chair.

"There's no such thing as *too* nice. This is just the tip of the iceberg. Wait until you see the rest of this place."

Will stepped out of the dugout and onto the field. Morgan followed. They stood near the first baseline and Morgan looked out on the stadium. It was massive.

"How many people does this place hold?"

"Seventy thousand. It's the biggest baseball stadium ever built. We should sell a lot of hot dogs!"

"That's a lot of fans. It's going to get really loud in here."

"You have no idea. Even when it's not loud, I'm going to make it loud. I had a crowd enhancer installed that magnifies the sound of the crowd. There could be two hundred people cheering in this place and I could make it sound like thousands. Wait until the visiting teams come to bat. It'll be so loud they won't be able to hear themselves think."

"I don't think you can play with the sound to work against your opponent," Morgan said.

"I beg to differ," Will said, smiling. "Follow me." They walked across the infield and into the visiting dugout. A cold-looking steel bench ran the length of the wall. It looked like a stretched-out prison cell.

"Are you still working on this one?" Morgan asked.

"No, it's done. This is what they get, the bums."

"I'm pretty sure you have to provide the same level of comfort for the visiting team as you have for the home team," Morgan said.

"This isn't Disneyland, Mr. St. John. They're lucky they even have a bench. I wanted to make them sit on the ground like dogs, but my lawyer told me I had to give them a bench. Go ahead, have a seat."

Morgan sat down. The hard bench was uncomfortable, like the bleacher seats at a small-town baseball field. Will took his phone from his bathing suit pocket. It was wet, and Morgan wondered if it would even work anymore. Will dried it off with the corner of his jersey.

"Are you ready?" he asked.

"Ready for what?"

Will touched his phone and grinned. "You'll see."

Morgan felt the bench start to get very cold—so cold that he had to stand up. "Whoa!"

"Isn't that awesome? On cold nights these suckers are going to freeze!"

"MLB won't approve of this, Mr. Panzell."

"Sit," Will instructed, his grin gone.

Morgan sat. The seat returned to a normal temperature. Will touched his phone again.

"Wait for it," he instructed.

The bench got warmer and warmer, and then red-hot. Morgan jumped off and Will laughed like a mad scientist.

"Again," Morgan began, "I don't think—"

"Sit," Will commanded. "You haven't seen the best part."

Will reminded Morgan of a spoiled child. He'd never before met an adult like him. Morgan sat once more. "This is the last time," he said. He sat for a few moments, wondering what was coming next.

Will looked at him, smirking. "The anticipation is killing you, isn't it? Let me set the scene. You just hit a home run. You trot around the bases and return to the dugout. You have a seat on the bench with your teammates. You think you're *so* cool. You're on top of the world, when..." He touched his phone and the bench collapsed, sending Morgan crashing to the concrete floor. "That happens."

Morgan looked up from his place on floor. Will held out a hand to help him up.

"I have to tell you," Morgan said, "I have some concerns about—"

"Stop being such a worrywart. Come on, we've got a press conference to attend."

Morgan allowed Will to help him up and followed him silently to the home dugout. For the first time in his life, he felt truly speechless.

Will stopped at another gumball machine in the dugout and popped a few more into his mouth. "What's the matter? You don't like gum?" he said, stuffing in even more.

"I'm fine, thanks," Morgan managed.

11

FULL-COURT PRESS CONFERENCE

The press room was jammed with writers, bloggers, and video reporters from around the world, all of them hoping to break the news of the Riptide's lineup. The room buzzed with excitement. All eyes were on Will as he and Morgan took the stage. Several microphones rested on a long table on a raised section of the room. Will stepped onto the stage and Morgan followed. Will waved and tried to thank the crowd for coming, but realized there was too much gum in his mouth. He tried using his tongue to jam it into the inside of his cheek, but it wasn't working. A little blue gum juice squirted out from his lips, landing on the table and the microphones. He coughed wildly.

The room went uncomfortably quiet. Finally, unsure of what else to do, Will took out his gum and stuck it under the table. The room let out a collective, "Eeeeewwwww."

"Oh, grow up," Will joked. His tongue and teeth were blue from the gumballs. "Like you've never seen a guy stick his gum under a table before. Right, Morgan?" he said, slapping Morgan hard on the back.

A few of the reporters scribbled in their notepads. Will cleared his throat, took a seat, and tapped one of the microphones in front of him. He leaned over and tapped harder on those in front of Morgan. One was covered in blue gum juice.

He cleared his throat again and said, "Thank you all for coming. Mr. St. John and I would like to take this opportunity to answer some of your questions and to talk about the exciting season we have ahead of us in the beautiful Lawrence Panzell Memorial Stadium. First, I want our fans to know we've been aggressive in accessorizing new players and adding them to the Riptide's lineup. First questions."

Every hand went up. Will pointed to a reporter in the front.

"Don't you mean 'acquiring'?" the reporter asked.

"That's what I said. We have been acquiring the very best players from around the sport to put together the most winniest team baseball has ever seen."

"I'm sorry. Did you just say 'winniest'?" the reporter asked.

"Yeah, I said winniest. With all due respect, I think it may be time to dewax your ears, sir." Will held his hand to the side of his head and pretended to clean his ear with a Q-tip. "They're called Q-tips. You should try one. They sell them at lots of stores." The other reporters giggled.

"I heard you fine, Mr. Panzell. I was talking about your use of 'winniest.' It's not a real word."

Will dropped his front teeth over his bottom lip like a half-human beaver and rolled his eyes. "Well, it is now, 'cause I just used it. Listen…we can sit here all day and have a lesson on vocabulary, Professor Boring-ton, or we can talk baseball! Who's got a b-ball question for Willster?"

The reporter sat, shaking his head in disbelief. Another reporter stood and said, "You say you've acquired the best players in baseball. How did you pull that off? Didn't players want to avoid coming to a team that has no history?"

"They may have been unsure at first, but I think they changed their minds when I got out the old checkbook." He held up his checkbook, waved it around like it was flying, and gave it a smooch. Then he leaned in way too close to the microphone and said, "It turns out big-time ballplayers like my big-time dollar signs."

Morgan noticed that the checkbook was wet from being in Will's bathing suit and wondered if he had even taken it out during his swimming lesson. It looked like he hadn't. Will called on another reporter.

"How did you convince Major League Baseball to allow you to start up a new team?"

"I think they saw my passion for the team. They know my dad was a huge fan, and I've seen a few games, so they figured, why not. Oh...and I have BILLIONS of dollars. I think that probably helped a little."

The reporter followed with, "It's well-known that your father was an avid baseball fan. It's charming that you've named the stadium after him. But did I hear you correctly? You said you've only seen *a few* games?"

"Did I say a few? I meant a bunch."

Morgan felt like he was in a bad dream. The reporters were turning on Will, and he didn't seem to realize it. The room buzzed with concern. Will called on another reporter.

"Do you feel you have the necessary skills to lead a professional baseball team if you've only seen a 'bunch' of games?"

Will shifted in his seat, clearly getting uncomfortable. "A few, a bunch, a bushel…what's the difference? The important thing is I've seen it before. It's basically the same thing over and over again—strike, ball, hit, strike out, touchdown, and so on and so forth. How hard can it be? My dad talked about it all the time. We're gonna be awesome! Next question."

Another reporter stood and said, "Mr. Panzell. There's a rumor that you're heavily invested in the Clear Coffee Company, which is on the verge of bankruptcy. Can you comment on that?"

The room fell silent. All eyes were on Will.

"No," he said. "Next question."

The damage was done. He called on a few more reporters, but they all asked him about his relationship with the Clear Coffee Company. Will stood abruptly, knocking his chair over.

"Stupid chair!" he mumbled, grabbing his knee. "I think I broke my knee. Morgan, go get me some ice."

Morgan, who hadn't said anything the entire time they were on the stage, said, "I don't know where anything is, Will."

"Fine! This meeting is adjacent!" he shouted. Before he walked out, he scratched the gum from under the table with his fingernails, popped it back into his mouth, and limped for the door. He tripped on one of the microphone cords and knocked over a garbage can. "Come on!" he shouted as he stumbled out of the room.

Morgan stayed on stage, facing the reporters, for another minute. He wondered what he had gotten himself into.

12

POST-PRESS CONFERENCE

February 15

Confused by today's press conference? You're not alone. I just watched it, and I can't believe what I saw. Will Panzell seems like a really odd guy. He didn't even share the lineup or any details about the team. I feel like it was some kind of a joke or something. I'll post again when I get a lineup confirmed.

13

THE CLEAR COFFEE COMPANY

The reporters turned their attention to Morgan. He apologized to them, explained that Mr. Panzell had been under a lot of stress, and said they would reschedule the press conference for another date.

That prying reporter had been right. Will was involved in a company called Clear Coffee. It's not an easy thing to lose billions of dollars, but Will managed to pull it off within months of his father's passing. Since he had so much money in the bank and invested, he was able to borrow all the money he wanted to build the stadium. His lawyers and accountants all advised him against it, but Will figured that once the season started, he'd make more than enough money to pay back the loans. By the time the stadium was finally completed, Will owed his banks close to a billion dollars .

Lawrence Panzell had left his accountants very strict instructions not to give Will a nickel more than was noted in the will. If Will lost or wasted it, there would be no rescue. For the first time in his life, Will was financially on his own.

For as long as Will could remember, he drank more than ten cups of coffee a day. He always suspected the habit yellowed his teeth. A five-year-old once asked him why his teeth were the same color as bananas. He became so self-conscious of his yellow teeth that he never wore anything white because it made his teeth look extra yellow. When he learned of a company planning to develop clear coffee, he couldn't help himself. He had to own it.

Clear Coffee was just that: *clear* coffee. It looked like hot water. When Will tried it for the first time, he couldn't believe it tasted exactly like coffee and had no color. He imagined all the people around the world who drank coffee but worried over their teeth, and he saw an opportunity to make a fortune. He bought the company from the creators and invested everything he had into building stores all over the United States.

Will kept his identity secret and ran the company quietly by making Ron the president. Ron did whatever Will told him. On Will's orders, the Clear Coffee Company served its coffee in clear cups. Will said it showed off the "clear-ee-ness" of the coffee. He also insisted that all four hundred stores be made completely of glass and clear plastic. The windows were clear glass from floor to ceiling; the tables, counters, chairs—and even the register—were all crystal clear.

People loved the idea at first, and the stores were very busy. But when customers put sugar, creamers, and milk in the clear liquid, it turned a pasty gray color. The combination of the clear cups and the milky liquid grossed most people out. Several employees of the Clear Coffee Company tried to warn Ron on several occasions that clear cups were a bad idea, but Will ignored them. He drank his coffee black, so his was always crystal clear.

The clear cups were only part of the company's problems. Some of the stores had problems with rat and cockroach infestations. Late at night, people walking by the closed stores could see the critters scurrying around in search of scraps. Someone videotaped a bunch of rats running around one of the stores late one night and posted it online. The video went viral and Clear Coffee was out of business as fast as it had started. Will was broke.

14

I ALREADY DO

After the press conference, Will returned to his office. Morgan followed, fielding e-mails on his phone. There were three phones in Will's office. All of them were ringing when they walked in. Will walked to the office's kitchenette. There was a coffeepot on the counter. Morgan assumed it was empty until Will poured a steaming clear liquid from it into a cup.

"Look at that," he said. "Crystal clear. Won't make your teeth yellow no matter how much you drink. The problem is, most people put milk or creamer in their coffee." He poured creamer into the cup and the liquid turned a gray color. "And this is what happens. No one wants to drink this gruel! Would you drink that?"

"I'm not much of a coffee drinker," Morgan lied, hoping to avoid the question.

"You had a coffee cup in your hand when you got here this morning. Don't be shy, Morgan. You can tell me. Would you drink this?"

"No. It looks pretty bad, truth be told."

"This stuff looks disgusting," Will muttered to himself.

"Excuse me," Morgan said. "My phone is ringing and buzzing like crazy. I've got to see who's trying to get a hold of me." He walked over to the couch and moved some of the mascot costumes out of the way so he could sit down.

Morgan listened to his messages. The first one was from pitcher Marty McGraw's agent, informing Morgan that Marty would no longer be playing for the Riptide, but would stay in San

Francisco instead. Morgan cringed. Marty was the best pitcher in baseball.

The second message was from Louis Elante's agent. His player had decided to stay with the Yankees. Louis was the best leadoff hitter in the game.

Morgan checked his third message; it was from an agent representing four of the top players in the league. He, too, was calling to say that his players would not join the Riptide as planned.

Morgan called the agents back. He explained that he was just learning about the team's roster and hoped there was a way to work things out.

Will was still in the kitchen rambling on about his coffee. He flung the cup of boiling-hot liquid over his shoulder. It landed next to the couch, almost getting on Morgan. Morgan had to slide to his right to avoid being scalded. He asked the agent on the other end of the phone if he could call back at a safer time.

"You almost got me with that, you know?" he said to Will.

"Sorry," Will said, punching the air. He threw his punch with such force, he lost his balance and stumbled toward his desk, knocking over a lamp. "I'm just so miffed at myself for thinking people would want to drink this junk. Jeez! I'm sick of the stuff and it's *my* company. I'm dying for a cup of *real* coffee. I haven't had one in months. *Shawn!*" he shouted abruptly.

The door to his office flew open and his assistant, Shawn, raced in.

"Run and fetch me a cup of the blackest coffee you can find," Will commanded.

Shawn was perpetually nervous and agreed with everything Will said. "Yes, sir, Mr. Panzell," he said.

"And clean up that lamp...someone broke it."

"You broke it while shadowboxing," Morgan pointed out.

"It was totally unbalanced. It's Shawn's fault. He put it there," Will said defensively.

Shawn didn't ask any questions; he scooped up the lamp and the broken pieces of glass and vanished out of the office.

"Sometimes coffee gets me a little amped," Will said sheepishly.

"I think 'a little' is a bit of an understatement. Are you ready to talk about what just happened in that conference? Or are you too jacked up on java?"

Will sat on his desk. "No, I'm good. What do you want to talk about?"

The question was so ridiculous, Morgan felt like he was dealing with a child. "Well, I think we should talk about what happened in that press conference back there."

"I don't want to," Will whined. "Let's play Xbox."

"No, we're going to talk about this. I've got messages from every major agent in the league telling me his players are not coming to the Riptide."

"Those reporters were out of line. They need to mind their own beeswax."

"Mr. Panzell, your phones are ringing off the hook. The few phone calls I already took were all from agents telling me their players will sign with other teams if you're broke. Please tell me you're not broke."

"I'm not broke," Will said seriously.

"Great! For a minute there, I thought you were really out of money," Morgan said, relieved.

"Oh, I am completely busted."

"Then why did you say you're not broke?"

"Because you told me to."

"Will," Morgan said, leaning in to convey the seriousness of the situation. "If you don't have the money to cut checks, then we don't have a team."

"But they signed contracts with the Riptide!"

"Yeah, but apparently their contracts had clauses allowing them to change their minds until opening day. If you're broke, I can guarantee they've all changed their minds."

Will couldn't believe that all his hard work and planning, which would have brought the best players at every position to the Riptide, was falling apart before his eyes. "So what are our options?"

Morgan picked up a baseball and tossed it to Will. "You're the big-shot billionaire's son. You tell me. Until today, I didn't even know who my players were. Now that I know who they were, they're gone. This isn't exactly going as you promised."

Morgan turned on the TV and switched to the MLB Network. The announcer said, "News is breaking fast and furious as deals are struck all around Major League Baseball. We're just now getting a look at the players Will Panzell lined up to play for the Riptide because agents and players are breaking their silence at news that the rookie owner is broke. It's an unprecedented day for baseball, and it looks like the Long Island Riptide has gone from an all-star team to a no-star team."

The other announcer said, "Yeah, this owner had a heck of a team lined up and it all just went down the toilet on him."

Morgan clicked off the TV.

"What are our options?" Will asked.

"What do you mean? Every player worth signing is on a team already, and if the news stories are right, you're dead broke. Players want to get paid." Morgan got the feeling Will expected him to find some magic solution. "Will, I don't know how else to put it. Spring training is in a week. Right now we don't have any players. I think the Riptide will have to sit out this season."

"No way! I didn't preorder half a million hot dogs and a river of soda and beer to sit the season out. This isn't fair," he wailed. "I mean, all these other teams have so much money. How am I supposed to compete?" Will fell to the floor like a child having a tantrum.

"Don't forget," Morgan said, "until yesterday, you were the guy with the golden checkbook, remember?"

Morgan had grown up poor. Everything he had in life he had earned through hard work and determination. He'd dreamed of a life in baseball from the time he was very little. Morgan had never been the best player, but he was always the hardest working. He struggled through Little League, high school, and finally minor league baseball before playing his way into the major leagues. He always understood the game better than most. After a fifteen-year career as a player, he bounced around the world working for teams as a batting coach, pitching coach, and just about every other job there was in baseball, except manager. He wanted to be the manager of a major league team more than anything. It was the final goal of his baseball career.

He took his hat off and scratched his bald head. "Can you pay my salary?"

Will looked up from the floor. "I cannot," he answered, standing up and walking over to the window, "but you're welcome to eat as many hot dogs as you can stomach, and you can sleep in your office during home games." He walked back over and had a seat next to Morgan on the couch. "Also, if we can get through the season, I should be able to make enough money in advertising to pay you double in October. What d'ya say? Do we have a deal?"

For the first time in his life, Morgan thought about quitting a job without having another one waiting for him. His mother had always told him never to run from a challenge, and he hadn't waited until he was seventy years old to start. So he shook Will's hand.

"I'll do what I can," he said.

"You won't regret it," Will replied.

"I already do," Morgan said.

15

SPORTS BLOGGER

Tommy watched the MLB Network and learned of the Riptide's problems. The announcers talked about all the talented players from around baseball that would have been on the team. They showed clips from Will and Morgan's press conference. They talked about how Will put his gum under the table and then back into his mouth. They talked about how Morgan remained manager, but no longer had a team to manage.

One of the announcers said, "I'd be surprised if they play at all this season."

Tommy shut off the TV and picked up his computer. He clicked on MLB.com and read more about Will's involvement in Clear Coffee and how much money he had lost. He clicked off the MLB site and logged in to his blog.

Tommy had started his blog the same day the Riptide's creation was announced. When he visited the Riptide website for the first time, it had a link for the press and bloggers to click. The link said that all bloggers were eligible for a free seat at the opening day game. Tommy quickly went to another website and created a blog. Then he went back to the Riptide's site and filled out all the information. Two days later, he got an e-mail with two free tickets to the opening day game. The name of his blog was written on the pass, along with his name and the words *sports blogger.*

16

THE DEAL

Morgan spent the rest of the day sending out e-mails and making phone calls in hopes of putting together a last-minute team. Will sat at his desk playing video games and complaining.

From all his years in baseball, Morgan had loads of connections and plenty of friends to call. "I'll do my best to get you a team, but you better figure out a way to pay these guys," he told Will. "And playing video games doesn't usually raise a whole lot of money."

"I do my best thinking when I play video games. I've got to figure out a way to pay back all the money I owe from Clear Coffee and finance our season."

"Were you playing video games when you decided to invest in Clear Coffee?"

"Ouch! That was a low blow, Mr. St. John, but I guess I deserved it."

"I'm just saying…I'm working overtime here and you're doing a whole lot of nothin'."

Will shut off his game and started to cry. He cried like a small child would cry. He pounded on his desk and grumbled something under his breath. Morgan watched in disbelief.

"Is this how you normally handle your problems?"

Will looked embarrassed, as if he'd forgotten Morgan was in the room. He wiped the tears from his eyes. "No. I don't usually cry. Babies cry. I'm not some big baby, you know."

"Whatever you say," Morgan said.

"I wasn't crying. My eyes were just watering. It's my allergies," Will said.

"You can call it whatever you like; just help me get a team together for the Riptide. We don't have time for your *allergies*."

Will blew his nose on the corner of his shirt and picked up the phone. "Here goes nothing," he said. He called every one of his dad's friends he could think of and begged for a loan. From what Morgan could tell, it sounded like they all said no.

After a few hours of dead ends, Will decided to call the one guy he knew would help him out: his dad's first partner, Montgomery Holmes. Montgomery was eighty years old and a self-made billionaire. Will knew Montgomery would bail him out, but he also knew he'd make him pay back every nickel.

"I'll lend you the money to run that team on bare bones," he told Will. "I'll even pay off all the loans you owe on that ridiculous coffee company. You'll agree to pay the players on your team the absolute minimum amount allowed by Major League Baseball, and you'll take no salary yourself. I'll cover bills like electricity, food, payroll for the stadium workers, and any expenses related to running the team. In return, you'll pay me back in full with an additional 20 percent the day after the season ends. If you're one penny short or a second overdue, I'll take it all. The team, the stadium, the TV contracts: everything becomes mine. If you really want this team to work, you're going to have to work for it. You agree to that, and you have yourself a deal."

"Can I make trades and pick up a few superstar players?" Will asked.

"Nope, everyone that plays for the Riptide must make the least amount possible. There will be no superstars on this team. In my day there was no such thing as superstar millionaire players. Guys made enough to get by and they played because they loved the game, not so they could drive a Bentley and sip champagne. And

I'll tell you something else: they could play circles around these nitwits today. If you want this team, you're going to have to earn it the hard way."

"It's a deal," Will said.

17

THE SCRAP HEAP

A week later, Will and Morgan met Charlie Night—Will's lawyer—in the stadium office "You've got half your problem solved," Charlie said. "We've paid off your debt on Clear Coffee and all the loans you owe on the stadium, but now you owe Montgomery Holmes a fortune. We've got the money to run the stadium, but there's no way you can take the Riptide south to Florida for spring training like you planned."

"We'll play in New York, then."

"It's the middle of winter," Morgan reminded him.

In only a week's time, Morgan had managed to convince enough players from his past to agree to play for minimum salary and on short notice. He told them all to report to the stadium for the first day of spring training on March 1. It was a late start, but the best they could do under the circumstances. He also told them that the plan was to take buses to the airport and fly to Florida for spring training. This was the first time he'd heard that they would not be traveling to Florida to play in warm weather.

March in New York is a cold month, sometimes the coldest month of the year, and that February it was also very snowy. Morgan had no plans of staying in the cold weather.

"Will, I know you're tight, but we should head down to Florida or somewhere warm to get these guys going. We can't play in this weather," Morgan said.

"Who needs warm weather? I think it's ridiculous that teams have to practice in warm weather in March. These guys are men. They can handle a little cold. I'm wearing a bathing suit, for goodness' sake."

"You're wearing a bathing suit because you're inside. I dare you to wear that outside."

"I'm not crazy! I'd get pneumonia."

"Teams practice in warm weather because you can't play baseball in the snow," Morgan said.

Looking out Will's office window, Morgan watched the grounds crew guy shovel out home plate. He looked like a poppy seed on a white blanket. "The players are going to be here soon. What am I supposed to do with them? They're expecting to get on a plane and fly to warmer weather."

"You'll have to figure something out," Charlie said, "because with our tight budget, there is no way this team can travel anywhere for spring training."

"We can practice inside the stadium," Will suggested. "Problem solved!"

"This isn't a joke, Will," Morgan said. "I've managed to convince players to believe in me and give your team a try. They're coming here today expecting to fly to Florida. Teams don't practice in the dead of winter. It doesn't make any sense!"

"No team has practiced in the winter until *now*, you mean," Will said. "We're doing it, and I'll tell you something else. It's going to be awesome!"

Down in the locker room, Shawn greeted each player and walked him to his player suite. When Will built the stadium, he'd been very wealthy and had spared no expense. Each player had his own small living room complete with a TV, computer, couch, and fridge. The shared player area had a bunch of flat-screen TVs, couches, pool tables, and Ping-Pong tables; it looked like it belonged in a hotel.

By the time Morgan and Will walked in, most of the team had already arrived. Will stood on a chair at the head of the room and announced, "Good morning, Long Island Riptide."

The guys kept hanging out. The room was so noisy none of them even heard Will. He took the wad of gum out of his mouth and threw it against the wall. The groundskeeper was standing behind him and said, "Come on, Mr. P; I've got to clean this place up."

"Sorry, Arturo," he said, halfheartedly trying to scrape it off the wall. It didn't work, so he left it. "You'll probably need a little peanut butter or something to get that off."

Ever since Will was a child, he'd had a habit of throwing things when he got frustrated. One time on a family trip he threw his favorite stuffed animal out the car window because his father was ignoring him. His father stopped the car, backed up, and got the animal. It was the first time Will successfully managed to get his father's attention. From that day forward—and not fully understanding why—whenever he got upset or really excited, Will usually threw something.

"Just try not to throw food," Arturo said. "I'm trying to keep this place clean."

"Understood, Arty. I'll try not to throw stuff anymore, but I'm not making any promises. It's an old habit." Will shifted his attention back to the players. They weren't paying attention to him.

Morgan put two fingers in his mouth and whistled louder than Will had ever heard. Everyone in the room turned.

"Wow! That was awesome. You have to teach me to do that," Will said.

The guys stopped what they were doing and walked over to Morgan and Will.

"Hey, fellas," Morgan said. "I would like to personally thank all of you for agreeing to come play on such short notice. I know you've all made sacrifices to be here and it means a great deal to me. I'd also like to introduce the owner and general manager of the Riptide, Mr. Will Panzell."

Will looked out over the group. "So, this is my team," he said. He got down from the chair and paced back and forth, sizing them up. He pulled another chair from a nearby table and stood on it, almost falling but regaining his balance. "This is the Long Island Riptide. This is my big dream come true, Papa!" he shouted. "Although, I have to admit, I don't recognize any of you. Are you sure this is the right group, Morgan?"

"Yeah, this is the right group," Morgan said, concerned that Will was about to insult the team. He moved in close and whispered, "It's not easy to get famous players when you can't pay them famous-player money."

"I understand that," Will said, loud enough for the guys to hear, "but these guys look like they should be collecting parking lot money or selling wieners and big foam hands." He got down once more, nearly slipping again. "OK, Morgan, you got me! Where's the real team?"

The guys mumbled to one another. Someone in the back said, "Is he for real?"

Morgan knew he had to stand up for his players and try to get the focus off Will. "Every one of these guys has played in the major leagues at one time in his career," he said, turning his attention back to the players. "Guys, my apologies. I'm really happy you made the trip, and so is Mr. Panzell. We hope you're ready for an amazing season."

There was a smattering of applause. Someone belched.

Will popped a few more pieces of gum into his mouth and got back on his chair. "Well, fellas, I guess this is what minimum salary gets me. As you know, you're the first men ever to wear the Riptide jersey. You should feel very proud."

"I don't," a voice from the back said.

"Who said that? Who said that!" Will demanded, losing his balance and falling off the chair, onto a table, and finally landing on the floor.

"Balance much?" another voice from the back said.

He stood up quickly and brushed himself off. Shawn fussed over him and said, "Are you hurt?"

"I'm fine. I meant to do that," he insisted.

"When do we leave for Florida?" a player asked.

"We don't," Will said. "Spring training will be in New York."

Morgan nearly had a heart attack.

The players started talking among themselves, sounding upset.

Morgan interrupted, saying, "Guys, as I explained on the phone when I talked with each one of you, this is going to be a strange season. We're getting a late start and we're behind on practice. We're thinking about staying here in New York so we're ready for the season before anyone else."

"Florida is overrated," Will said. "I was there once as a kid and it was super humid and stuff. This is where we need to practice. You guys can settle in to the Lawrence Panzell Memorial Stadium and begin enjoying its awesomeness." He noticed there were six kids in the group. "Why are there kids in here?" Will asked.

A large man wearing a tank top and a winter hat pulled down over his ears said, "These are my kids. We're gonna be staying at the stadium, so we'll need seven beds and a bunch of pillows and blankets and stuff."

"You can't stay here!" Will announced. "This isn't a hotel."

"Morgan?" the man said.

"It's OK, T-Bone. Shawn will get you and the boys whatever you need. Shawn, please take T-Bone and his sons and help them settle in."

"T-Bone?" Will asked. "What kind of name is T-Bone?"

"It's my name," T-Bone said. "You got a problem with my name?"

The guys got very quiet. One of the kids stepped forward—he looked about three or four—and said, "Yeah, you got a problem with my dad's name?"

Will looked around and realized he'd said the wrong thing. "Of course not. When I was little they used to call me W-Bone," he lied. "I just—"

Morgan interrupted, "Listen. For now, everyone just get settled in. I'll explain about spring training later on. If you need anything, let me or Shawn know and we'll get it for you. We may not be paying much, but I think you'll agree that the stadium is pretty phenomenal." The guys nodded. The player area was nicer than anything they'd ever seen. They weren't making superstar money, but it sure felt built for superstars.

"Who else is planning on living in the stadium?" Will asked. Every hand went up. "Come on, Morgan!" he complained.

"You want a team or not?" Morgan asked.

"Fine, but understand that this stadium was built with the very best of everything. It was built to be the best, for the best. Not for you guys. You guys are lucky to be here to enjoy it. Don't mess the place up."

A tall guy with his hat turned backward interrupted, saying, "I'm going to pitch, right?"

"I don't know. Are you a pitcher?" Will asked, frustrated by the interruption.

"No, I'm a left fielder, but I've always wanted to pitch."

Some of the guys started walking away, and a few were on the phone or checking their e-mail.

"Why not?" Will said, exasperated. "We've got a team full of disrespectful wash-ups. We might as well let the left fielder pitch. While we're at it, why don't I let my dog play catcher?"

"I'm only asking because Morgan already promised me I could. I'm just confirming it with you. If I can't pitch, I'm on the next plane back to Puerto Rico."

Will knew he didn't have the time to find new players and had to work with the ones he had, so he said, "I don't know; talk with Morgan. He's the manager."

"You'll pitch," Morgan confirmed.

"That's all I care about," the man said, and turned to walk away.

The rest of the players started heading back to their suites, too. Will sat in his chair and Morgan pulled his own up next to him.

"Morgan, what's the deal with these guys? Why aren't they psyched up? Are you guys psyched up?" Will yelled. There was no reaction from the players.

"I'm psyched for a nap," someone yelled.

Morgan leaned in and whispered, "You give a manager a week and no money to put a team together, and this is what you get. These are the best players I could convince to play for us. They may not seem like much right now, but I'm telling you—there's a lot of potential in this room."

"Potential for disaster. Can they even compete?" he asked.

"I think you should be happy they're here. Let's worry about competing another day," Morgan answered.

18

WIFFLE BALLS

Morgan ran his first indoor spring training practice the next day, March 2. The guys ran up and down stairs, they raced from one end of the stadium to the other, and they practiced catches in hallways. Morgan used every indoor part of the stadium he could.

He left the guys for a lunch break at noon and went up to Will's office to talk. Shawn served the team hot dogs and sodas from a concession stand.

When he walked into the office, Morgan found Will asleep on the couch. He sat next to him and said, "Wake up. Will, we can run cardio and throwing drills all day inside the stadium, but we need to practice hitting at some point."

"They can hit outside, can't they? It can't be that bad out," Will said, rubbing his eyes and sitting up.

"Have a look," Morgan said.

Outside, the bleachers were covered by at least a foot of snow. The air was blustery with blizzard conditions.

Will glanced toward the window. "I think it looks doable," he said.

"Come on, Will. We can't have guys hitting in a blizzard. How do you want me to practice hitting?"

Will thought for a moment and then went to his closet and yanked open the door. It was full of baseball gloves, bats, and hats. He rummaged around in the closet and finally held up a big bag of Wiffle balls. "Here! Have the guys practice in the entry of the stadium. The ceilings are high, and there's plenty of room."

"You can't be serious! You want a Major League Baseball team to practice hitting with Wiffle balls?"

"No, I want *this* team to practice hitting with Wiffle balls. They could probably practice hitting with snowballs and it wouldn't make a difference, because these guys are a bunch of bing-bongs. My old man would never have approved of this group."

"Will, any time you bring together a bunch of guys who've never played together on a team, it's not going to be pretty the first few days."

"Oh yeah? I bet if you put Derek Jeter, Ryan Howard, Adrian Gonzalez, and a bunch of other all-star players together and had a practice, they'll look pretty good."

"That's not fair. First, we're not an all-star team. Second, you have a team practicing inside a stadium in the middle of a snowstorm. We should be in Florida!"

"You're right; it's not fair. We *were* supposed to have the best team in baseball, and we're stuck with a team full of schlubs," Will said. "Do you realize we have a ten-thousand-pound man on our team? This isn't football or that samurai wrestling, you know."

"I think you mean sumo wrestling."

"Whatever. Why is he here? And why does he have six kids living in his suite?"

19

T-BONE STAKE

The "ten-thousand-pound man" Will was talking about was T-Bone Stake. He didn't weigh ten thousand pounds. He weighed three hundred and seventy-five and stood six feet nine inches tall. His real name was James Stake, and in his prime he'd been a power hitter known as T-Bone Stake. They called him T-Bone because he ate a T-bone steak before every game. He was a very good first baseman. He fielded well for a man his size and could hit with power. He played for a short time in the majors as a member of the Royals, but experienced most of his success in Japan. T-Bone led the Japanese league in home runs two different times in his career.

He was living in Arizona with his six kids when Morgan called. He hadn't played professional baseball in five years.

Right before Morgan called, T-Bone was on the phone with the bank. They'd said he had three months to pay up on his mortgage or he would lose his house. T-Bone needed the money, so he had to come out of retirement.

He agreed to play for the Riptide as long as housing was provided. Morgan explained that housing wasn't in the budget, but the stadium was amazing and he could live in it if he liked. During their call, T-Bone mentioned neither his six kids nor his weight. He decided he could better explain it in person. He asked Morgan to fax a contract so he could sign and send it back right away. He also insisted on a guarantee that he would be the starting first baseman.

"I start every game at first base, Morgan. No way I'm playing second fiddle to another guy. I waited a long time to play in the bigs again, and I'm going to be a starter if I come back."

"Whatever you need, T-Bone. I'm just happy to have you on the team."

"Fax the contract," he said. "We're on our way."

"Who's we?" Morgan asked.

"Don't worry about it. We'll be there."

20

THE PITCHING LEFT FIELDER

The left fielder who asked Will if he could pitch was Owl Perz. In his prime, he'd played left field in the minor leagues and the Caribbean league.

He was selling hot dogs at a stadium in Puerto Rico when Morgan called. He answered the phone, jammed it between his ear and shoulder, and continued to work on the dogs.

"Owl, it's Morgan St. John. How've you been?"

"Who?" Owl replied, squirting mustard on a chili dog.

"You played for me in the Caribbean league a few years back."

"Don't remember," he said.

"I spent a season trying to teach you how to throw a slider."

"Still not ringing any bells."

"I paid your rent the last month of the season. You used to call me the Old Man."

"Oh yeah, Morgan. What's up, Old Man?"

"I'm the head coach of the new expansion team in New York called the Riptide. I know it's last minute, but I wondered if you might want to join the team. We could use a good left fielder. Are you playing in a league right now?"

"Yeah, Morgan. You could say that," Owl said, glancing around the baseball stadium. He squirted mustard on two more dogs. "I'm down here in Puerto Rico. I'm slinging mustard." The crowd cheered because a player on the field singled.

"Slinging mustard? You mean you're finally pitching?"

Owl didn't mean he was pitching, but slinging mustard sounded like a pitching term so he went with it. "Yeah, man, I'm slinging some crazy mustard down here. I'm slinging some crazy hot mustard. You should see me." He handed the hot dogs to a man at the front of the line, took his payment, and made change. There was another hit in the game and the crowd cheered.

"It sounds like things are going great for you down there, but what do you say? Will you come up north for an old friend?"

"I'll come if I can pitch."

"I'll send a ticket. Just promise to bring your hot mustard."

21

YOU'RE STILL A LOSER

Tommy came home from school on March 4 and clicked on the TV. The guys on the MLB Network were talking about the Riptide.

"There are rumors that they aren't even going to play the season," one guy said.

"They're going to play. I can confirm that. I'm just curious to learn who they're going to put on the field," another guy said.

"There are reports that the team is practicing in the Lawrence Panzell Memorial Stadium.

How a team practices in a foot and a half of snow is beyond me. It just proves how crazy this Will Panzell guy really is," a third announcer added.

"I know. This guy must be completely out of his mind. He's invested hundreds of millions of dollars in a stadium, but where's the team? I don't know how he plans to build a fan base. If I'm a fan, I don't even know who my team is!"

Tommy clicked the TV off and took out his computer. He logged on to his blog.

March 4

Wondering what's going on with the Riptide? You're not alone. Opening day is only a few weeks away and still no one knows a single member of the team. Curious? Me too, that's why I want season tickets for my birthday. I'm talking to you, Grandma and Grandpa.☺

He stood up to put the computer away and realized he had gum on the back of his jersey. After school, Tommy was already in his bus seat when Chris got on. Chris had slapped Tommy on the back as he walked by—which Tommy found odd—and said, "Hey, Tommy! Still rooting for the Riptide?"

"Yep," Tommy replied.

"Then you're still a loser," Chris said, and continued walking to the back.

The gum was stuck in the same spot where Chris had slapped him on the back. Tommy tried to get it off by washing it in the sink, but it wouldn't come off. He took off the jersey and threw it into the laundry. *Hopefully it will come out in the wash,* he thought. He wanted to tell his parents, but decided not to. It was late and they were tired from being at work all day.

22

T-REX AND GOGGLES

The next day, Will met more of the players. The first person was Michael Lehan. Michael was six foot six but had very short arms. The combination made for an interesting fielder. He was very good at catching line drives, but he had a hard time throwing the ball. He could only throw to first from second base.

"Wow! I didn't know we had a T. rex on the team," Will said, hoping for laughs from the other guys in the room.

"That's not cool," someone said.

"I'm kidding, but look at those arms. Watch. Do a jumping jack."

"OK, it's time to go, Will," Morgan said, taking him by the arm and pulling him out of the area. A few players booed Will out of the room.

When they got in the hall, Morgan said, "You can't talk to people that way. He's your player. Why are you making fun of the guy?"

"I didn't," Will insisted.

"I was standing right there. You told the guy with the tiny arms that he was like a T. rex."

"Did you get a look at him?"

"Yes. He's a very good second baseman. He played for me in the Caribbean league. He's a sensitive guy. Don't make him self-conscious, and he should be fine."

"Can we put T. rex on his jersey?"

"No!"

"Can I have a guy in a T. rex suit run around the stadium when he's up? I'm going to do it. The fans will love it."

"No, they won't. That's a terrible idea."

They walked back into the player area and Morgan waved over Don Tapper, who was on the couch watching a movie. Don had extremely thick eyeglasses. He was legally blind without them. He had to tilt his head up all the time to keep them from sliding off his face.

Don bumped into a large garbage can on his way to meet Will. "Sorry," he said to the can, thinking he'd bumped into a person.

"What in the world is this?" Will asked.

"This is your center fielder," Morgan said proudly.

"Look at the windshields on this guy!" Will said, shaking his head in disbelief. "Are you looking for leaks in the ceiling?"

"No, why?"

"Because you keep looking up."

"I'm looking up so my glasses don't fall off."

"May I ask why you need such thick glasses? While I'm at it, why don't you have a pair of those sports goggles?"

"I don't like goggles. They make me look like a frog. These are my lucky glasses. I have to wear them because without them I am pretty much blind."

"Morgan, you can't be serious! How can I have a center fielder that can't see?"

"He's very good," Morgan said defensively, feeling concerned that Will was about to insult another player.

"I have a sense for the ball," Don said.

"I'm getting a sense right now, but it's not for the ball. I'm getting the sense that my team stinks!" Will said.

"Excuse us, Don," Morgan said, leading Will out of the player area again and back to Will's office.

Neither of them spoke for a few minutes. Will busied himself by putting on a chipmunk costume.

"Morgan, we haven't known each other long, but I have to ask you a serious question," Will said.

"What is it?"

"Are you a crazy person?"

"I might ask you the same question."

"I counted on you to deliver a team to me, and you give me these clunkers?"

"You promised me an all-star-quality team to manage before I moved back here from Japan, and you gave me nothing. I had a pretty good thing going on my last team. I left because I thought you knew what you were doing. Instead, I'm at spring training in a blizzard and my players are practicing with Wiffle balls."

"Excellent points," Will said, putting on the chipmunk head and taking a look in the mirror.

"Why are you wearing that?"

"We need a mascot. I'm trying to find the right costume."

"Aren't we the Riptide? What's a chipmunk got to do with a riptide?"

"Nothing, that's the problem. The costume place sent over all these suits, but none of them make any sense for our mascot."

"A riptide is a dangerous water current that sweeps people out to sea. Why don't we make our mascot a shark or some other water creature?"

"Excellent thinking, Morgan," Will said, taking off the costume. "I've got to head down for my lesson with Miss Kathy. I'll see you later on. While I'm gone, please figure out a way to make this team stink less."

23

THE SLEEPY CATCHER

About an hour later, Will walked in to where the players were practicing. He was sopping wet. Morgan was watching video of some of the players. The guys were playing Wiffle ball and the radio blared loud rap music. Will stood next to Morgan's chair, dripping. A puddle formed at his feet.

"Why don't you grab a towel?" Morgan asked.

"I forgot one and I couldn't find Shawn. I'm freezing. Let's meet a few more of these dopes. Who's left for me to meet?"

"Your catcher. Please don't call him a dope."

"If he's anything like the other misfits, I'll call him whatever I like."

There was a guy on the floor sleeping with a catcher's bag under his head like a pillow.

"Let me guess, that couch slouch is my catcher?" Will asked. "Morgan, am I on one of those hidden camera shows?"

"This sleepy bear is Chaps, our catcher. He's excellent behind the plate." Then, under his breath, Morgan added, "When he's awake."

"What do you mean, 'when he's awake'?"

"He suffers from a sleeping disorder. He sleeps a lot."

Chaps bolted up. "Who's there?" he mumbled.

"Holy sheet cake!" Will exclaimed. "I'm doomed."

24

MORE GUM ON THE JERSEY

Tommy's trouble with the guys on the bus got worse. His mom knocked on the bathroom door as he scrubbed gum off his jersey for the second time that week. "I'll be out in a minute," he said.

"What are you up to in there?"

"Not feeling that great," he said, which was mostly true.

He wasn't sick in the way his mother assumed. He was sick of *it*. He was sick of the teasing, the cruelty, and being the nice guy all the time. When he was younger, being nice was rewarded. Parents and teachers made a fuss over him and praised him for how nice he was. Now, being nice was a liability. His good behavior made him a target, especially on the bus. It was why Chris and his buddies had all stuck their gum on his Riptide jersey as he left the bus.

He came out of the bathroom in his undershirt and tucked the wet Riptide jersey under his arm.

"Did you get something on your jersey?" his mom asked.

"Yeah," Tommy said. "I was just rinsing it in the sink so it won't stain."

She took it from him and ruffled his hair. "You're such a responsible kid. Do you know that?"

"Yeah, Mom."

"Dinner's just about done. Why don't you get going on your homework?"

Tommy's dad came through the front door and dropped his stuff on the kitchen table. "What's the deal with that new team? They were talking about it on the radio all the way home."

"I guess they've been practicing for spring training in the stadium on Long Island. The owner doesn't have enough money to take them to warmer weather," Tommy replied.

"Have they announced any of the players yet?"

"Nope. There are all kinds of rumors, but no one seems to know for sure."

"Yikers! Maybe asking for season tickets for your birthday was a mistake," Tommy's dad said.

"No way. I can't wait for opening day. You guys said I can take the train on my own. You mean it, right?"

"Yeah," his dad said, "if you're comfortable with it. It's only two stops and you'll have your cell phone. I used to take the train from here to the Bronx when I was a kid."

Tommy had heard about how his dad took the train on his own when he was very young, and how they didn't have cell phones back then. His dad told him the story every few days. He still wondered if his parents would really let him take the train by himself. He figured it couldn't be any more dangerous than the school bus.

25

RIPTURD

While the Riptide practiced inside the stadium with Wiffle balls and tried to survive the snow, the rest of the major league teams practiced and scrimmaged in warm, tropical climates. In the week leading up to the start of the season, websites and newspapers had a field day poking fun at the Riptide. On March 25, Morgan released the final roster to the press. The next day, one newspaper headline read simply: RIPTURD.

Tommy researched the roster as soon as it was posted online and wrote about the players on his blog.

March 25

Starting lineup for the Long Island Riptide: Season 1. Some say Ripturd, but I say Rip-It-Up!

- *Adrean Bellmin, Right Field*
- *Michael Lehan, Second Base*
- *Chris Mossey, Third Base*
- *James Stake, First Base*
- *Chaps Logan, Catcher*
- *Don Tapper, Center Field*
- *Jorge George, Left Field*
- *Jeff Zeen, Shortstop*
- *Owl Perz, Pitcher*

This lineup may look pretty weak to some, but I've done some research online, and I'm pretty excited. Most of these guys have played for a long time. If you add it all up, the team has over two hundred years of experience on their side. So while some reporters are bashing the Riptide, I say this team has potential. Can't wait for opening day!

Did you know James (T-Bone) Stake hit forty-seven home runs two years in a row in the Japanese league, and he was only twenty-six when he retired from baseball? He's my player to watch this season.

26

EDGES

Toward the end of March, the weather warmed and the players were finally able to get outside and practice. With all the guys living and sleeping in the locker room, the place was a mess.

Will hardly slept the night before the first game. He wanted desperately to make his father proud. He knew that once the season started, he only had until October to figure out a way to make enough money to pay Montgomery

Holmes back. His dream of owning a major league team had finally come true, but it looked pretty unlikely that he'd keep it more than one season.

The morning of the first game, Will held a meeting a few hours before the team took the field. "As you guys may or may not know, I've fallen on some pretty tough financial times."

"You're paying us the least amount of money allowed by Major League Baseball," the T. rex said.

"We've been practicing with Wiffle balls," Chaps added.

"You sleep in the conference room, your manager lives in his office, and most of us players live in our suites," Chris, the third baseman, said.

"Excellent points, gentlemen. All of these things are true, but that's because it's the only way I could afford to run the stadium. I know I've been a bit of a handful since you've been here, and you guys were probably expecting a lot more. The challenge before me is to make this team profiteral. It's the only way to keep it going and to avoid selling it off after the first season."

Morgan interrupted, saying, "You said 'profiteral.' I think you meant *profitable*."

"Did I say profiteral? I thought I said profitable."

"No, you said profiteral."

"That's weird! I don't even know what a profiteral is," he said.

Jeff Zeen googled it on his smartphone. "I think it's some kind of fancy dessert."

"What are you talking about?" Will asked. "I am trying to tell you I need to make money with this team or it's all going to be over. Today we open the season against the New York Yankees. Does anyone know the difference between them and us?"

Adrean raised his hand.

Will said, "Yes…person I haven't met yet."

"I'm the right fielder. We met about a dozen times."

"Don't remember, doesn't matter. What do you think? What's the biggest difference between them and us?"

"They're good?" Adrean said.

"No! I mean...yes, of course they're good. They're the Yankees, for crying out loud. But there's something else!"

"We've got nothing to lose and everything to gain?" a distant voice said from one of the bathrooms down the hall.

"You're close, mystery voice," Will hollered. "Who said that?"

"It was that guy Arturo that's always cleaning up after you," Michael, the second baseman, said.

"Arty, I'm talking with the team!" Will shouted. "Oh, and when you're done, there's a cheeseburger stuck to the big screen in my office that needs your attention. I'm not sure how it got there!" he lied. Shifting his attention back to the team, he said, "Guys, I'm a...well, *was*...a wealthy man. I used to be a billionaire.

I've lost over one-point-two billion dollars in my lifetime. I'm a businessman, and I *mean business.* I'm going to do everything in my power to make sure you guys win. There is *nothing* I won't do to win."

"What can you possibly do for us? We're the ones on the field," Owl said.

Morgan interjected, "What I think Mr. Panzell means is that he can offer us support and encouragement."

"No, that's not at all what I meant. Baseball is serious business, gentlemen, and if there's anything my late daddy taught me, it's that when doing business, you need an edge. This stadium gives us more edges than an…um…quick, somebody give me a shape that has lots of edges."

"A rectangle," someone said.

Will made a disappointed face. "That's a really bad answer. It's only got four edges."

"A square," someone else said.

"Seriously! You guys can only name four-sided figures? Nobody took geography in school?"

"An octagon," Morgan said, "and you mean geometry. Geography is the study of land, Will."

"Ohhh," the guys all said.

"That's why this guy's the manager. His head is totally jammed full of brains," Will said. "This team has more edges than the biggest octagon you've ever seen."

"What does that mean?" T-Bone's son asked.

"T-Bone, why is your kid here and talking at a meeting?"

T-Bone stood up and crossed his arms. He was massive. "Because I told him he could."

"Fair enough," Will said. "Well, T-Bone's kid—"

"My name is Kevin," the boy said.

"OK, Kevin. What I mean by the octagon analogy is that we have more edges than the other teams."

"I've been on a million teams and every owner has some bull shark idea of how he's going to make the team better," T-Bone said. "I have news for you, Mr. Panzell: We aren't very good, and you can talk all day long and make speeches about edges, but it ain't gonna make us any better."

"Think quick," Will said, tossing Adrean a ball. He didn't react, so it went soaring over his head and bounced down the hall. "Nice catch, Babe Ruth. Clearly, we don't have an edge in the talent department. It's not your fault, though. You guys were born average players. But we've got advantages other teams don't have."

"Like what?" Adrean challenged.

"Like this," Will said, pushing a button on his phone.

The guys could all hear voices coming from the phone.

"You bought us phones," someone said.

"No! I'm broke, remember?"

"It's just a bunch of people talking," T-Bone said.

"Wrong again. Listen."

"Is that the Yankee dugout?" Morgan asked, concerned.

"YES!" Will said. "I have the opposing team's dugout and locker room wired. I can hear everything they say. Let's listen to their game plan."

"You can't listen to what they're saying. That's cheating," Morgan said, snatching the phone from Will.

"No, that's called having an edge! Give it!" he shouted, trying to pull his phone out of Morgan's hand. The two struggled for control of the phone.

27

GET ON THE FIELD

Morgan instructed the team to get dressed and meet him out on the field. He walked Will back to his office and told him to stop listening in on the Yankees.

Tommy was already on his way to the stadium on the train. His parents had warned him countless times about strangers and talking with people he didn't know. The funny thing was that his parents didn't think twice about putting him on the school bus, where he was harassed and teased daily. Compared to the bus, the train was a walk in the park. There was even a guy riding the bus who was in charge and checking tickets. Tommy was pretty sure if anyone started picking on someone else, that guy would stop it. He wished someone like that was on his school bus.

When the train came to a stop at the stadium, Tommy couldn't believe his eyes. It was massive. The train station was in the stadium, and when he got off it was like being in a mall. There were stores and food places everywhere. He followed the signs for the field. At the entrance gate, he proudly displayed the blogger badge the team sent him. One of the attendants showed him to his seat. It was in the press section, about ten rows behind home plate. The team was already on the field taking batting practice.

Tommy was thrilled. Baseball was his favorite thing in the whole world. He loved everything about it. The stadium felt like home to him.

The team had sent him two tickets to the game. His coat covered the other seat to make it look like someone was sitting there and would be back soon. His mother told him to do it so he wouldn't have any trouble with strangers. She and his dad were working and couldn't go with him. She didn't love the idea of him going alone, but she knew how much he wanted to go and so agreed to let him go anyway.

"Why don't you invite a friend?" she had asked.

"I don't mind going alone. I'll be concentrating on the game and working on my blog," he said.

"Is it that you don't want to take a friend? Or do you not have anyone to ask? I can call up one of my friends and find you a playmate," his mom said.

Tommy had friends, but he didn't have anyone he really connected with enough to want to spend an entire day with them. His mom liked to set up playdates with the people she worked with. Most were from other towns, and Tommy wasn't really interested in meeting kids in other towns.

One time she dropped him at this kid's house who wanted to watch movies all day. He loved westerns and made Tommy watch them from the time he got to his house to the time he left. He wouldn't just watch them, either; he talked through the whole movie, telling Tommy all about the actors and where the movie was shot. Tommy called him the Outlaw because he was always dressed in full cowboy stuff. He wore a hat, boots, and even a holster.

One time he spent the day with a kid that hit. No matter what Tommy did, the kid hit him. He told the kid's mother that he wanted to go home, but she just laughed and said, "Oh, you're fine, Thomas. Your mom will be back soon enough."

Drew's house was the worst. Tommy always had to deal with his love-crazed sisters. They called him their prince. The whole time, Drew usually played video games, his mom texted her friends, and Tommy hid from the sisters. One time they had friends over, too, and the girls took turns proposing to him. He must have said no a thousand times. They made him a paper crown and kept trying to put it on his head.

Being alone at the game was just the way he liked it.

Tommy was amazed at the stadium. It was everything Will Panzell had promised. It was brand-new, had great views from all seats, and there were food vendors all over the place.

He noticed a bunch of windows hanging just above the left field, right field, and center field fences. Above each set of windows was a sign: INDESTRUCTIBLE WINDOW COMPANY. Beneath that, the sign read, "OUR WINDOWS CAN'T BE BROKEN."

He took out his computer, which they let him take into the stadium because he had a press pass, and wrote a post on his blog:

April 7

Opening Day! The stadium is amazing! There are windows hanging above the fences. It's pretty cool. I wish the windows weren't inde-structible, because it would be cool to see a home run that busted a window.

The team is out on the field. They are starting to practice their hitting. It's going to be an interesting game today. Thanks for the seats, Riptide.☺

Interesting fact: Owl Perz once said in an interview that his favorite place to pitch was the backyard of his house growing up, because there were big trees by the fence and no one could ever hit a home run against him.

28

THE GUYS IN
THE BOOTH

The Yankees finished their batting practice and Tommy put in his earphones so he could listen to the local sports radio station. The announcers—Ken, Roger, and Jerry—talked about the mess Will Panzell had made for Major League Baseball and the players.

"They are by far the biggest embarrassment for baseball since Pete Rose got caught gambling," Ken said.

"This is a perfect example of why you can't just let any guy with a load of money and a dream buy a baseball team," Roger added. "It takes insight and understanding of the game. None of which Will Panzell possesses."

"Well, like it or not, fans," Jerry said, "the Long Island Riptide seems here to stay, for this season at least. We can argue all day long over whether they should be allowed to play their season with the team they've put together. The fact is, it's a beautiful day for baseball and the game is about to get under way."

"The stadium is gorgeous but mostly empty, and I can't say I'm surprised," Roger said. "The team the Riptide is putting on the field is a farm team at best. I think my son's middle school team could beat these guys. Some people around baseball say they're the worst team, talent-wise, ever put on a professional field."

"Yeah, I'm one of those people," Ken added. "There's a line between an owner running a team with little talent and what Will Panzell is trying to do, which is to put a talentless team on the field."

"It's certainly going to be interesting to see how it all shakes out," Jerry said. "Well, regardless of how you feel about them, the Long Island Riptide seems set to get this season under way. The Yankees are ready to go. Owl Perz is on the mound for the Riptide today. He's a pitcher that bounced around the Caribbean league for most of his career, and rumor has it he was selling hot dogs when Morgan St. John, the manager of the Riptide, called and asked him to join the team."

"Yeah, there are pitchers like this guy bouncing around leagues all over the world," Roger said. "I took a look at his numbers, and I just don't understand why they signed him. He was a left fielder for most of his career and just utilized every now and again as a relief pitcher. How he has come to be the opening day starter against the New York Yankees is beyond me."

"I'm speechless," Ken added. "Absolutely speechless. I know he had a relationship with

Riptide manager, Morgan St. John, but I don't know why they signed him. Get ready for a long season, folks. This has the makings of a real disaster."

"Well, all that being said, let's see what the Riptide has in store for us. Perz appears ready with the first pitch. He winds up and it's a strike called. About ten people are clapping for the call. Everyone else in attendance appears to be a Yankee fan," Jerry said. "That one was right over the plate. If he throws like that all day, the Yankees are going to hit quite a few balls into the seats," Jerry added. "Here's the pitch. It's a line drive into left field, base hit. Wait! The Yankee batter, Julian Monroe, took a few steps out of the batter's box and just fell to the ground on his way to first. The left fielder, Jorge George, throws across the diamond to first base and the runner is out at first. Can you believe that? What a strange way to start the season!"

"I don't believe it. Monroe is still down on the ground, too. What happened there? He had a base hit and then on his way down the line, he fell to the ground like a lump. I bet he tore his Achilles because he's still down. I remember when I was a player—" Ken had been an all-star player for many years in the big leagues and loved nothing more than to tell stories about when he was a player. The other guys had been instructed by the show's producers to change the subject whenever Ken brought up an old story.

"No, Ken, Monroe is up now," Jerry interrupted. "He appears to be upset about the call. He's giving the umpire an earful."

"The umpire is waving him off the field, and rightly so. You can't complain about falling on your face," Roger said.

The small crowd cheered. Will watched from his office window. He listened to the Yankee dugout on his phone.

Tommy sat in the stands taking notes on his laptop. His grandfather texted him: *You get there OK? How's the stadium?*

Tommy texted back: *Made it fine. The train was a piece of cake. Stadium is amazing. I'll post about it later on when I get home.*

His grandpa's reply text message was: *Have fun!*

The second batter came up. He tapped his bat on the plate, spit, and got in his stance.

Jerry made the call from the booth: "The pitch is on its way—it's another one right down the middle. Strike one. Owl Perz is looking pretty good out there so far. He's really moving fast here between pitches, too. The windup—and the pitch is on its way. It's a ball. So, one ball and one strike to the batter. Here comes the third pitch from Perz: it's a rocket to the gap between center and right. The center fielder is moving over, but he won't get there, it's in for an extra base hit. This one will roll all the way to the wall. The runner is headed for second base. Wait, what's this? He's down on the ground, too! The center fielder, Don Tapper, throws it in to second. The second baseman, Michael Lehan, runs over to the runner and tags him out. Two outs. What is going on down there, Ken? Have you ever seen anything like this?"

"I can't say I have, but the runner is pretty worked up right now. He's getting into it with the second-base umpire, and I can't figure out why. These Yankee runners can't seem to stay on their feet."

"He's headed back to the dugout now," Jerry announced, his voice growing with excitement. He's pointing to the dirt as if there's something wrong with the infield. If I'm the Yankees, I just want to concentrate on staying on my feet right now. Boy, oh boy, what a way to start. So Perz has two outs and he's ready to deal to the next batter."

The batter, Frankie Bass, stepped into the batter's box. The first two pitches were strikes. The third pitch was a meatball right down the middle. He was about to swing when a pain struck him and sent him to the ground. The umpire called strike three.

When Frankie was a kid, he'd once been hit in the foot with a dart. The pain he felt now reminded him of that dart. He waved his arms to the umpire and argued that something was wrong. The Yankee manager came out on the field and argued with the umpire to keep his player from being thrown out of the game. He had no idea what he was arguing about until he got a shock in his legs that made him jump in the air.

Tommy couldn't believe his eyes. He almost wished he had someone with him to talk it over with. Instead, he took notes for his blog.

Weird stuff going on in this game. Players keep falling down and pointing to the ground. Not sure why they're so upset.

The guy in front of him turned around and said, "What's the deal out there?"

Tommy shrugged and said, "Maybe bees?"

"Naaah," the guy said. "You'd be able to see bees. This here's something strange."

A small model of the stadium sat on a table next to the window in Will's office. Before the infield was constructed, Will had electricians wire the entire field. When Will touched any part of the stadium with a special metal pointer, a mild shock was delivered to anyone standing on that part of the field. He got the idea while playing the game Operation. He had just delivered a shock to Frankie Bass. He watched out his window as the Yankees argued with the umpire.

The umpire finally threw the manager of the Yankees out of the game and warned the Yankee players to "Cut out the nonsense!" They tried to explain that they didn't know what was happening. The umpire yelled, "Play ball!"

Nothing strange happened again until the fifth inning. The Yankees were winning six to nothing; they were up, with the bases loaded. The cleanup hitter, Anthony Dasbi, was at the plate and the count was two balls and two strikes. Perz threw a strike right down the middle and Dasbi was in midswing when a jolt of electricity zapped his feet. Strike three was called and Dasbi fell to the ground. Dasbi yelled at the umpire. "Something's not right! I just got shocked!" The umpire again waved him back to the dugout.

Morgan was up on the steps of the Riptide dugout, feeling suspicious. The announcers talked about it in the booth.

"I'm not sure what's going on here, Roger. It seems like the players on the visiting team are experiencing some kind of problem," Jerry said.

"Yeah, it's figuring out how to simply stand up," Ken said.

"They're flopping around like a bunch of fish," Roger added.

Ken began, "This one time in Seattle, I lost my balance rounding third—"

"That sounds very interesting, Ken, but we need to go to commercial," Jerry interrupted.

The umpires huddled up in the infield and tried to figure out what was going on. One of the umpires held the bat and pretended to be a player in the batter's box. Of course, nothing happened because Will didn't press the button.

During his team's at bat, he laid off the buzzer so his guys could get good at bats. Even so, each player on the Riptide struck out in order.

By the top of the seventh inning, people's eyes were glued to the game. The Internet sites buzzed about the game's events, and ESPN carried live coverage of the game. The first Yankee batter of the sixth inning managed a single with no problems, but when the second player came to bat, the zaps started again.

The Yankees called their players off the field and filed a protest. The game was cancelled because the Yankees manager would not allow his team to continue until Major League Baseball figured out what caused the shocks.

On the train ride home, Tommy finished his blog post.

Later on, when his parents got home from work, he said, "You guys aren't going to believe this, but the game was cancelled early because there was some kind of crazy thing happening with the Yankees."

"What was going on?" his mom asked.

"The Yankees kept falling down and arguing with the umpires. They told reporters they were getting shocked. It was crazy!"

"That sounds awful," she said. "I have good news, though. You have a package from your grandparents."

Tommy hoped it was season tickets. His grandparents had been talking about getting them for him all winter long. He opened the box and pulled out the newspaper stuffing. Packed inside were a new Riptide jersey, a train pass, and a season ticket.

29

BUZZ

A very upset Morgan came to Will's office after the game. "What went on out there?"

"It's called an edge. I just needed to make sure it worked correctly. Man, that was fun! Wasn't it?"

"No! It was embarrassing, Will! I didn't sign up for the circus. I signed up to manage a big-league baseball team. What happens when they find out you can listen in on the visiting team's dugout?"

"Oh, they won't find my recording device. It's hidden too well. There's one in our dugout, too, you know? Careful what you say about me down there, Morgan. I can hear everything. I can eavesdrop on just about any part of this stadium with the click of a button. I even have devices at the hot dog stands. I like to hear what the fans are saying—and let me tell you, they were talking up a storm today."

"Of course they were talking! The players on the field were being toasted."

"Wasn't it wonderful?"

"No! It was completely unprofessional."

"Oh, don't be so dramatic. Where's your sense of fun? They weren't in any danger. The voltage was set very low. And we have BUZZ now." He clicked on the TVs on the wall of his office. Each one was on a different channel, and each program talked only about the Riptide."You know what they say, Morgan?" Will asked.

"No, what do they say?"

"There's no such thing as bad press. This is a great thing for us."

"I just hope this is your last 'edge.'"

"Yeah, it's my last one," Will smirked.

30

WALK-OFF HOME RUN

Major League Baseball scheduled a double-header the next day and released a comment saying that the events of the game the day before could not be explained and were under investigation. During the remaining games at the stadium with the Yankees, Will didn't zap anyone because investigators from the league were there and he didn't want to blow it. The Riptide lost both games of the doubleheader and the final game of the series to start the season with three losses and zero wins. Tommy went to all three games. He didn't mind that they were losing; he was excited to be a part of something new.

After the three home games, the team hit the road on April 11 for their first road trip. Will had to budget the money for the team very carefully. He couldn't afford to send them by plane or luxury bus. He bought an old school bus and the guys piled inside. Will didn't travel with the team because he had some work to take care of at the stadium.

The team went on a ten-day road trip. Morgan was happy to have the team away from Will and the stadium so they could get a taste of playing without Will's "edge."

On their road trip, they won one of the ten games. Their record was one and twelve to start the season. They had the worst record in baseball, and attendance was looking very low for their upcoming nine home games.

The next three home games were against the Reds. They were all night games, and Tommy's parents let him go. The Reds had a hitter named Tim Went who led the league in home runs. He hit a home run in every game of the young season. In two games, he hit more than one homer.

Tommy was halfway through his first hot dog in the top of the fourth inning. The Riptide had a two-run lead. There were two men on base and Went was up to bat. Tommy listened to the guys in the booth through his earphones.

"Here we go, folks. Let's see if the Riptide can keep their lead here against the biggest bat in baseball. The pitcher is ready to deliver his first pitch. It's a fastball drilled to the corner in left field. This ball has a chance of going out. The left fielder, Jorge George, is moving back to the warning track. This ball looks like it's going out. Wait, he makes the catch with plenty of room," Jerry said.

"Did you guys see what I just saw?" Ken asked.

"The wall moved!" Roger exclaimed. "The wall in left field just moved back a few feet, giving Jorge George enough room to make the catch."

"I don't know what's going on in this stadium, folks, but if I didn't just see that with my own eyes, I wouldn't believe it happened."

"Yeah, something's funny all right," Roger said. "I've been working in baseball for over thirty years, and I've never seen a wall move!"

The umpires huddled at home plate, pointing and trying to figure out what had happened.

"Did the fence just move?" the head umpire asked.

The third-base umpire said, "It moved, all right. Saw it with my own eyes. That ball should have cleared the fence easily."

The manager of the Reds came out on the field and argued. The umpires ordered him back to the dugout and called for a review of the play.

While they were off the field reviewing the video, Morgan turned to one of the bench players. "Did that fence just move?" he asked.

"I think it did!" the player answered.

Morgan was furious.

The umpires came back on the field after about ten minutes of review. They had rules for the ball hitting the foul pole, rules for fans interfering in a play, and rules for just about every other situation you can think of, but they did not have a rule for a moving fence. "The batter's out!" the head umpire announced. The manager of the Reds went berserk and was thrown out of the game. The few people in the stands buzzed with excitement.

Morgan knew Will was probably listening to the dugout from his office. "Call me, Will! I know you can hear me," he said. The phone rang a few seconds later. He picked it up, "What are you doing?"

"It's called an edge, Morgan. I'm an octagon, remember?"

"How did you make the fence move?"

"The fence didn't move. You must be seeing things," he said, and hung up.

Morgan hung up and threw the pack of sunflower seeds he was holding. The bench player said, "He's got something to do with this, doesn't he? That guy is crazy."

"I heard that, bench player!" Will piped in from somewhere.

"Sorry, boss," he replied.

"I hear everything, kid. Watch your step or I'll have you selling hot dogs by next inning."

Tommy wrote notes as fast as he could.

The fence in left moved about three feet back and made it easier for Jorge George to catch the ball. I can't believe it was called an out. I wonder if that's ever happened before in MLB history. Seeing the Riptide is never boring. I can't believe so few people are at the stadium to see this.

Everything calmed down until the seventh inning. T-Bone was up. He got an inside fastball just in the spot where he liked it. He swung and connected. The ball soared for the corner in left field. It was going to be close. Everyone leaned in to catch a glimpse. As the ball sailed for the fence, the wall moved in four or five feet. The Reds' outfielder, not looking at the fence, ran straight into it and fell to the ground.

The ball just made it over the fence. The crowd—if you could call it that—went crazy. The Reds players yelled for the umpires to do something. The head umpire made the home run sign and wondered what he was going to do. He'd seen the wall move.

In his office, Will danced and pumped his fist. The Reds walked off the field and the game became the second protested game of the season.

31

THEY THINK YOU'RE A LUNATIC

After the game, Morgan didn't speak to Will. He locked himself in his office to think over what to do. He met him early in the morning the next day.

"I don't know how you can sit there with a huge smile on your face and look all relaxed after what happened yesterday," Morgan said.

"Yesterday was awesome. We have been getting coverage on every sports channel from here to Honolulu. It's a beautiful day out. The weather is starting to get warmer. My ticket sales are through the roof. Tickets have been selling like crazy for tonight's game. We'll have our first sellout. Seventy thousand tickets sold! We keep this up and I'll be able to pay Montgomery back early. I might even be able to pay your salary. You should be thanking me."

"People aren't coming to see a baseball game. They're coming to see a circus. Everyone loves a circus, Will."

"That's not true. I hate the circus. Clowns give me the creeps."

"You know what creeps me out, Will?"

"No, tell me."

"What creeps me out is all the crazy things you're trying to do with this team. First you're listening to the other dugout during games, then you're zapping players on the Yankees, and yesterday you had *moving fences*. What's next?"

"It's funny you should ask that," Will said.

When Will rose, Morgan saw that he had on half a shark suit. Will reached into a large box behind his desk, took out the top half, and put it on. He held the shark head under his arm.

"I read something online," Will said, "that mentioned Owl Perz said he used to love pitching in his yard because he could get batters to hit the ball into the trees, which blocked the ball from going over the fence."

"You didn't," Morgan said, frantically racing to the window.

Morgan's blood pressure spiked when he saw there were forty-foot evergreen trees planted throughout the outfield and along the home run fence.

"You know you can't plant trees in the outfield, don't you?" Morgan said, feeling defeated.

"Shawn!" Will shouted. "Please send Chaz in."

A smaller person, also wearing a shark suit, walked in and took off his shark head. It was Charlie Night, Will's lawyer. "Hello, Morgan," he said, holding his fin out for a shake. Morgan reluctantly shook his fin.

"Do you like our new mascot costumes, Morgan?" Will asked.

Morgan didn't answer; he was too mad to think about costumes. "Charlie, are you aware of all the crazy stunts Mr. Panzell is pulling around here?"

"I can't comment on said accusations because I don't know what you're talking about," Charlie said, winking at Will.

"Have a look. He's planted trees in the outfield. We're going to have another protest game today. He can't do this."

"Actually, it says in the rule book that the owner of a team may design the layout of the field to his or her liking. He or she may also make minor changes as necessary."

"I'd say planting trees in the outfield is a MAJOR change. Can you think of one other ball field that has trees in the outfield?" Morgan asked.

"No, I can't," Will said, "and that's why we're doing it. Now, grab a shovel. I have a few more trees I'd like to put in before the game starts. We'll need your help." He handed Morgan a shovel.

Tommy got to the game early and couldn't believe his eyes when he saw the trees in the outfield. He took a few pictures and uploaded them to the blog.

As game time approached, people started to fill the stadium. It was the biggest crowd yet for the Riptide. Will's crazy antics drove ticket sales and interest in the team.

The umpires walked out on the field and the manager of the Reds was already fuming. They called Morgan over as soon as he walked out of the dugout.

"You can't have trees in the outfield," the head umpire said.

"Tell me about it. I'm just the manager. You need to talk with the owner. He's the one who planted them," Morgan said. He pointed out to left field where a man in a shark suit was digging.

Tommy sat in his seat, typing about the situation on his computer. The stadium buzzed with energy. People pointed at the trees, took pictures, and speculated about what the trees might mean.

A small gold golf cart drove in from the outfield. A shark sat in the driver's seat. From the height of the shark, Morgan figured it must be Charlie Night. The lawyer waved his fin at the crowd.

"I don't know what goes through the mind of Will Panzell, folks," Roger said from the booth.

"He's planted trees in the outfield. Things with the Riptide have just gone from weird to flat-out crazy," Jerry added.

"Yeah, it's getting to be kind of disturbing, guys. This guy isn't just a little crazy. He's a full-blown loon. Who in their right mind plants trees in the outfield of a baseball field?" Ken ranted.

"There's plenty of commotion down on the field now as the managers and umpires talk it over. There's also a man in a shark suit in on the conversation," Roger said.

"Of course there is," Ken added. "Why would that surprise you here at Lawrence Panzell Memorial Stadium? I'm sure it's just the beginning of the weirdness we'll see today."

Will walked over to the mound where everyone was meeting. He took the shark head off and the crowd reacted as soon as they realized the Riptide owner had come onto the field. Half the crowd cheered wildly; the other half booed. Soon all the fans in the stadium were on their feet.

"They love me, buddy!" Will shouted in Morgan's ear.

"They think you're a lunatic!" Morgan replied.

"Hey, they paid for the show. So I'm going to give them what they want," he said. "Dance class is now in session. Feel free to join in if you can keep up."

The umpires tried to talk to Will as he hopped and danced around.

Charlie Night clapped his hands and chanted, "Go, Will! Go, Will!"

Will was on the ground trying to complete his back spin, which was made very difficult due to the large shark fin on his back, when the head umpire said, "Mr. Panzell. You need to start acting like an owner here! This is madness! We can't play this game with trees in the outfield and you're about to have seventy thousand angry fans on your hands."

Will stopped trying to spin and stood. "You're right about one thing: those are definitely trees in the outfield. But we can most certainly play this game. You're here, there are players here, and the kids in the crowd are cramming hot dogs into their yappers. I say play ball."

"The commissioner says we can't play a game with trees in the outfield," the head umpire said.

Will put his arm around Charlie and said, "Under this shark head is my lawyer, Charlie Night. He will explain all the legalese to you gentlemen while I continue busting a move for my fans." Will moonwalked away from the umpires.

Charlie took off his shark head and held out his fin. "Gentlemen, I'm Charlie Night and I'm a lawyer. Allow me to explain why this game is going to be played."

In both dugouts, the players on both teams looked on in shock at the unfolding events.

"I've played for some crazy owners before, but this guy is hands down the craziest," the T. rex said.

"Who?" Owl asked.

"The owner," T-Bone said. "He's out of his mind."

"Oh yeah, that guy's completely nuts. Why are there trees in the outfield, anyway?" Owl asked.

"I heard it's because you said you used to keep the ball in the field when you were a kid by pitching to the trees," T-Bone's son Kevin said.

"You gotta be kidding me. I said that in an interview over ten years ago."

Out on the field, Will did the worm. The crowd tried to get the wave going. Tommy could hardly keep up. He posted pictures and wrote about what he was seeing as fast as possible.

On the field, Charlie explained that there was nothing in the rule book preventing an owner from putting in trees. "Gentlemen, I'm very good at finding ways around rules. There is nothing in the rule book that says we can't do this. In addition, the contract we signed with MLB gives us complete control over what goes on in this stadium. We play this game or I'll file a suit against Major League Baseball on behalf of the seventy thousand people here today. The game is scheduled to begin at seven o'clock. It's six fifty. I suggest you all go take a wee so you don't have to go during the game. Tell the commissioner to read his contract a little closer before trying to cancel a Riptide game again." He put his shark head back on and said, "If you'll excuse me, I have a Douglas fir to finish planting in left field."

The umpires called the commissioner, who talked with his lawyers. They realized Charlie Night was right. The way the contract with the Riptide was written, Will *did* have the legal right to make the changes. The umpires were instructed to play the game, trees and all, while the commissioner's office figured out what to do next.

"Well, folks," Ken said, "I've officially seen it all. We are about to play a Major League Baseball game with trees in the outfield."

32

TREEMENDOUS

This is the coolest thing I've ever seen. The game is being played with trees in the outfield. They're lined up along the outfield fence and are high enough that someone would really have to blast the ball a mile in the air to get it out. It kind of reminds me of playing baseball at home. The stadium looks like a big backyard with all the trees. It's going to be hard for the outfielders not to run into them.

It looks like the team mascot is going to be a shark. The owner and every stadium employee are wearing shark suits today. I feel kind of bad for the vendors who are trying to work with their hands in fins.

Tommy listened to the announcers on the radio as he typed.

"The fact that we're playing this game is by far the strangest thing I've ever seen in my thirty years of watching and playing baseball," Roger said.

"You know," Jerry said, "the kid in me thinks this is absolutely fantastic, but the adult in me can't believe how insane it is to have trees in the outfield."

"Where's the commissioner on all this?" Ken asked. "The league really has to find a way to get Will Panzell under control. It's only May. What other crazy plans does this guy have for the league?"

"I don't know," Roger said, "but we're about to get under way."

The game was both very confusing and exciting to watch. Balls flew into the trees and players couldn't get to them. Balls bounced off trunks and rolled in crazy directions. There were three inside-the-park home runs in the first four innings. In the fifth inning, David Fern, a Reds player, hit a monster shot into the trees. It fell to the ground and he managed to slide into home for his second in-the-park homer of the day. The team celebrated out on the grass. Fern high-fived all the players on his team before returning to the bench. When he sat on it, the bench collapsed. Half of the Reds team, as well as the manager and several coaches, went crashing to the ground. The Reds manager pulled his team from the field and filed a protest against the Riptide with Major League Baseball. Seventy thousand people booed, although it sounded like even more because of Will's crowd enhancer.

After the game, Will talked to the reporters in the player area. "The last time I checked, this was baseball. It's played in yards all over the country. Where's the fun in the game these days? We all know the history of baseball. It was started by a couple of cavemen with a stick and a rock who were just trying to have a little fun." He called on the first reporter.

"That's not the case at all," the reporter said. "Baseball was invented by Abner Doubleday. He lived in—"

"I'm not interested in a lesson, Professor Nerdington. The point is, where's the fun? Why does the game take itself so seriously? It's baseball," Will preached.

"Mr. Panzell, you put trees in the outfield of a professional baseball game today! Why?"

"I read an article saying that Owl Perz loved pitching when he was a kid because he could get guys to hit the ball into the trees. The trees kept guys from hitting home runs against him. Before the season even started, I told my players that I'd do anything to win. I want to give them every advantage I can."

Tommy listened to the radio interview all the way home. When he got there, he clicked on the TV and the guys on MLB were going absolutely crazy.

"The league should shut this team down once and for all. These guys aren't fit to play professional ball, the owner's got more nuts than a fruitcake, and worst of all, he's making a mockery of the entire sport."

"I can't believe he actually put trees in the outfield. The commissioner of Major League Baseball must be out of his mind right now. I mean, where do you even begin with this guy?" another announcer asked.

A third announcer interrupted, saying, "We just got a statement from the commissioner's office that Major League Baseball is going to have a hearing for the owner of the Riptide later in the week. As details emerge, we'll keep you informed."

33

NO ONE WAS
ELECTROCUTED

The next day, Major League Baseball held an official review of the Riptide and Will's actions. Several executives and the commissioner of baseball sat in front of microphones on a stage. Will sat facing them, at a small table with a single microphone resting on it. He wore his shark suit. The head was in his lap.

The commissioner said, "Mr. Panzell, as you know, we're all here to review and discuss your actions in the three protested games against your team. I'll start with the opening day game against the Yankees. After further review, we've come to learn that you were electrocuting players on the opposing team. This caused them to fall to the ground and fail to play."

Will leaned in, "Electrocuted is a harsh word, Mr. Commissioner. I'd like it strucken from the record."

"Mr. Panzell, this is not a court of law, and you mean stricken."

"Whatever you just said, that was what I meant. I don't like that you're saying I electrocuted the Yankees. It's kind of an exaggeration."

"I'm in charge here, sir! I will call it whatever I wish. Are we clear?"

"There's no need to get all hot under the collar. I'm just saying, nobody was electrocuted. It was more of a mild shock."

"Please do not speak unless I ask you to speak."

Will pretended to lock his mouth and then throw away the key. A few reporters tried to hold back their laughter. People usually treated the commissioner more seriously. Will's attitude stunned the people in the crowd.

The commissioner called the head of fields and grounds to the microphone. He reported that he had inspected the stadium the day of the incident and found that the Riptide stadium was wired in a way that allowed Will to deliver a shock to any part of the field from a miniature version of the stadium in his office.

"Mr. Panzell has controllers installed in his office that allow him to deliver a shock to any part of the field. He also has a device in his office that allows him to move the home run fence in or out," the man reported.

The commissioner spoke directly to Will. "Mr. Panzell, we allowed you to create this new expansion team because we believed you had the resources and character to take on the challenge. Here we sit, just weeks into the season, and you have caused so many problems for the league that it's hard to believe. Your father was always a great baseball fan. I don't think he would have approved of the childish antics you've brought to the great game of baseball. I've decided to fine you personally for the disruptions you've caused. I'm also ruling the protested games as losses for the Riptide—and if I have to speak with you one more time about cheating in any form, you will no longer be allowed to enter your own stadium. In addition, I will ban you from every major league stadium in the country. Are we clear?"

"Does that include teams based in Canada? They aren't in our country," Will smirked.

The commissioner looked furious. "Yes! That includes Canada. I will ban you from baseball for life! Do I have your word that you will behave and follow the rules?"

"Yes," Will said, crossing his fingers inside his fin.

34

CHARLIE AND THE CHOCOLATE BAR

After the hearing, Will behaved himself to avoid getting banned. Attendance at the games dropped dramatically. The team continued to lose games all through June, July, and August. Will spent money—Montgomery's money—while making almost none of it back. He was on track to lose the team. Montgomery Holmes couldn't wait to take over. Will knew he had to figure something out quick if he was to have any chance of keeping the team.

He and Morgan were having lunch at the Panzell Panini Hut before a four o'clock game on a hot August day. Will looked out over the tens of thousands of empty seats as the team took batting practice and the grounds crew worked on the field.

"I don't know how to pack this stadium given the players we have. I was hoping to create a buzz and fill this place. I owe a lot of money, Morgan, and I have to pay it all back the day after the season ends."

"It's one thing to create a buzz and another to break the rules," Morgan said.

"Why does everyone keep saying that? I gave them a little shock. No one knows how to have fun anymore. I still can't believe they won't let me have trees in the outfield. If there's grass, why not trees? It doesn't make any sense."

"What we need is a buzz that doesn't involve cheating. You need to find a good clean reason for people to root for this team. I know they're capable of playing better under the right conditions. Who knows? If we get some positive things going around here, they just might get on the right track and win a few games before the season ends."

"What about a flash mob?" Will exclaimed. "You know what a flash mob is, right? When hundreds of people start dancing all at once."

"I know what a flash mob is. I don't think it's a good idea, though," Morgan said. "You need an idea that's actually going to create more fans of the team."

"We could have a pretty cool flash mob in this place. Imagine it, Morgan: five or six hundred people dressed in shark suits, dancing at the same time." Will held his hands up as if he were framing a picture. "In the middle of a game, all the guys that walk around the stadium selling stuff could break into a dance. The hot dog guys, the big foam fellas, even the security guards. It would be SOOOOO AWESOME!"

Morgan wrung his hands. He knew Will well enough to know he would go through with the idea. He needed to get him focused on something else—quick. He said the first thing that came to mind. "If you really need to fill this place that bad, we're so far out of the playoffs already that you might as well hold some kind of raffle and let the winner play left field for a day or something."

Will beamed. Morgan started explaining another thought, but Will interrupted him. "Stop! Shhh! Don't say another word." He threw the rest of his sandwich across the room.

Arty saw it land on a seat and said, "Come *on*, Mr. Panzell."

"Sorry, Arty," Will said. "I'm having a flash of genius. I'm a little excited right now." He leaned in and whispered to Morgan, "That guy is always on me about throwing my food."

"Maybe you should stop throwing your food?"

"Don't be ridiculous. I love throwing stuff. It helps relieve stress."

"Not for Arty."

"Very funny. Seriously, I think you just figured it out, Morgan. We'll have a raffle. Better yet, we'll hide a special card in a pack of baseball cards, like they did with the golden ticket in that movie *Charlie and the Chocolate Bar.* The person who gets the special card will win. And the winner won't just get the chance to play for a day, Morgan. The winner will get the chance to start in left field for the rest of the season. I'll let the winner pitch, sing the national anthem, and tap dance if it puts tushies in the seats."

Morgan felt that he'd just made a very big mistake. Still, he didn't bother trying to talk Will out of the idea. Will was far too excited to be convinced that it was a bad one.

35

THE LEATHER CARD

A few days later, the contest was announced. Media coverage was unbelievable. Every news show talked about Will's contest. Will appeared on all the late-night TV shows and accepted interviews by countless reporters. Tommy read about it on the Riptide website. People from coast to coast bought up baseball cards in hopes of playing in the big leagues.

"I can't believe this!" Tommy exclaimed. "Mom, check this out," he said, pushing his laptop in front of her. "The Riptide is giving away one special card and whoever gets it wins a chance to play on the team for the rest of the season!"

She took the laptop from him and read:

Mr. Will Panzell, owner of the LI Riptide, is holding a contest to find his next left fielder. Mr. Panzell placed one special leather card in a regular pack of baseball cards. The person who finds the card will win the opportunity of a lifetime: a chance to play on a Major League Baseball team. The winner will travel with the team, live with the team, and play on the team. Good luck, baseball fans.

"How can they do that?" his mom asked. "Are they really so bad that they would allow just any-one to play for them?"

"I guess so. The last game didn't even have a thousand people in the stadium."

"How many games have they lost?"

"Their record is the worst in baseball. They're on track to be the worst ever. The 2003 Tigers have the worst record in history. They were forty-three wins and one hundred nineteen losses. The Riptide's record is worse than the Tigers' was in August of that season."

"So why do you go to every home game?"

"Because I'm a fan. I love that they're new. I think they'll get better over time, and I can know that I believed when no one else did."

"That's sweet, Tommy. Imagine if you won that contest!"

"The chances are nearly impossible. There's only one card. It will be like finding a needle in a haystack."

At the stadium, Morgan and Will sat in Will's office.

"How can we really manage this thing if we get just any old player out of the stands?" Morgan asked.

"Don't worry about it. This is the idea that's going to get me out of debt. I can feel my dad looking over me. This is going to work. Who knows? Maybe the person we get will be amazing. It sure can't get much worse than what we have."

Morgan knew that it could absolutely get worse, but he didn't say anything.

36

FRENZY

The days that followed were complete lunacy. Every store selling baseball cards sold out of its entire stock. People bought as many packs as they could get their hands on. People sold unopened packs on eBay for hundreds of dollars.

To sell tickets to the games, Will announced that every ticket holder would be given a pack of cards at each home game until the leather card was found.

The upcoming home games all sold out in a few hours. The stadium was packed for every game in their series against the Pirates. Unfortunately for Will, people bought tickets, went to the game to get their cards, and then went home after the first couple of innings. By the ninth inning of each game, the stadium was almost completely empty. He couldn't believe people took their cards and didn't even stay to watch the game.

"I don't understand this," Will complained to Morgan in the second inning of a game against the Pirates. "We sold out tonight and the stadium looks like a ghost town…"

"People only want the cards, Will. Look on the bright side: at least you sold the seats."

"Yeah, but we have sixty thousand hot dogs to sell. I need to find a way to get people to buy the tickets and then stay at the stadium and buy junk. I need money, Morgan. I need it fast!"

"They just might stay and watch the game when someone wins the contest."

The team lost that game 14–0. Will held a meeting in the locker room afterwards.

"This is bad news," Will said. "We're selling out every game, but people aren't staying and spending money on hot dogs and other useless items."

"Maybe the contest is a bad idea and we should stop?" Owl said.

"That's no kind of attitude for a Riptider. We're getting folks in the door; we just need to figure out how to keep them here. Tonight was a sellout, but the place was empty by the second inning. No one wanted to stay and see the base-ball game."

"How about putting an actual baseball team on the field every night?" one of T-Bone's sons said.

"In case you haven't noticed," Will replied, cracking open a soda, "we do put a team out there every night."

"I wouldn't call them a team. They are men in baseball uniforms, but I wouldn't go as far as calling them a *team*."

"What are you rambling about? We have a team," Will said. "A spammed good one, too."

"They're not good. The only reason anyone comes is to laugh at them and get your cards. It's a joke."

Will looked defeated. "I can't pull any more stunts or I'll get banned from the league. Who's got an idea? A legal idea?"

No hands went up. Will threw his soda against the wall. It almost hit Arty.

"Come on, Mr. Panzell!"

"I'm sorry, Arty!"

37

FINGERS CROSSED

Tommy continued to blog every day about the team and the card hunt. He used his savings to buy a pack of cards each day. The card store near his house had a huge supply of packs, but only sold one pack per customer a day. They knew Tommy and put a pack aside for him each day. Every time he hoped to find the special card inside, and imagined how amazing it would be to put on a major league uniform and play on a major league team.

38

THE PACKAGE

On a rainy Saturday morning, Tommy's mom asked him to bring the garbage cans in and get the mail. The rain felt refreshing on his bare feet. He purposely stepped in a puddle on the way down to the mailbox.

Chris and Antonio pedaled in his direction. He hadn't seen them since school let out at the end of June, and he'd been enjoying the break. He tried to open the mailbox and grab what was inside before they reached him. They were zooming down the hill faster than he realized;

before he knew it, they had raced through a puddle, splashing him with muddy water. Black spots of muddy water stained the back and side of his Riptide jersey.

"Loser!" they shouted as they pedaled off. Tommy grabbed the mail and the tiny box inside and sprinted back to the house.

When he got inside, his mom said, "How many times have I asked you to put on your shoes before going outside?"

He shrugged. "Too many?"

"Too many is a good answer. May I have the mail, please?"

"Here you go," he said, and ran for the laundry room in the basement. When he got there, he took off his jersey and threw it on the laundry pile on the floor. He raced back upstairs and was on his way to his room when his mom said, "Hey, you have a package here."

"Really? Is it from Grandma and Grandpa?" They were the only ones who ever sent him packages.

"I don't know. It's not a Florida return address, but maybe it's something they ordered for you."

Tommy took the small package and gave it a shake.

"Who were the boys you were talking with outside?" she asked. "Do you want to invite them over for a playdate one day?"

Tommy made a face. "Not exactly."

"At least they're active. Not many kids are outside playing on a wet day like today. You need to get outside more and get some fresh air."

"I get plenty of fresh air. I go to every Riptide game and they're all outside. I don't like riding bikes around in the rain. It doesn't make any sense." He pulled the top tab off the package and shook out the envelope inside. He tore open the envelope and found a pack of baseball cards in it.

"Who's that from?" his dad asked, walking into the kitchen.

"I don't know. There isn't a receipt or a note inside."

"It's got to be from your grandparents. Why don't you call and thank them?"

"OK," Tommy said, and picked up the phone to dial. "It's kind of weird that they didn't include a note or anything."

"They probably just forgot. You know your grandparents," his dad said.

"Yeah, but the address is a New York address," his mom added. "If they sent it, wouldn't it be postmarked from somewhere in Florida?"

"Hey, Grandma," Tommy said after she answered, "thanks for the baseball cards you guys sent me."

"I didn't send you any cards, sweetie," his grandmother said. "Let me ask Grandpa if he sent them." She shouted, "Harvey! Did you send Tommy a pack of baseball cards?" There was a pause, and then she said, "They're not from us, honey. Thank you for the call, though."

"No problem, Grandma. I'll talk with you soon."

"OK, sugar. I look forward to reading your blog later. Good luck with the cards. Who knows, maybe the leather card is inside. Put your mother on, please."

Tommy handed the phone to his mom. He took another look inside the box and read the address. He couldn't figure out who the cards were from.

"Open them," his dad said, sipping his coffee.

"OK, here goes." He pulled back the plastic wrapper and shuffled through them. There was something thick in the middle sticking to the other cards. He also realized there were only six or so cards in the pack instead of the normal ten. While his mother yammered away on the phone and his father returned to eating his breakfast and reading something online, Tommy dropped the wrapper and most of the cards on the floor.

A thick card remained in his hand—*THE* card. The one made from baseball glove leather.

"Um…Dad…" he said.

"Yeah, pal?" his dad said without looking up.

"I think I found it."

"Found what, son?"

"I think I found *it*!"

His dad looked up from the computer. Tommy read the card:

Congratulations! You're the winner and this is your ticket to the bigs. As the holder of this card, you are now a member of the Long Island Riptide baseball team.[1] Please call the number on the back of this card in order to receive further information and learn more about this amazing opportunity. On behalf of everyone at the Riptide, welcome to the team. We hope you can play left field![2]

You're welcome!

Will Panzell

1. *This card is nontransferable; you may not sell or trade it.*
2. *Winner agrees that he/she accepts salary decided upon by us. Amount listed in number 3 below.*
3. *$0.00 (zero dollars).*

His mom hung up and noticed the card in Tommy's hand. "Oh my gosh! What is that?"

"It's *the* card!" Tommy's dad exclaimed, knocking his coffee over as he jumped up from his seat.

"I'm not sure what's happening," Tommy said, stunned. "Is this really happening?"

They were so excited that even the dog, Cracker Jacks, barked.

"Stop barking, Cracker Jacks," his mom scolded.

"It's real," his dad said after snatching the card from Tommy's hand.

"Here," his mother said, shoving the phone at her son. "Call the number on the card! Cracker Jacks, stop!"

39

W-43-I-52-LL-543-IZ-
5954-DA-591-M-797-AN

Tommy dialed the number. After three rings a man answered. "Hello," he said.

"Hi," Tommy said nervously. His parents were inches from him, trying to listen in on the call. "I'm calling about the card."

"Sorry, but I know not of what you speak," the man said, in an obviously fake British accent.

"I think I won the player contest. I have the leather card."

"Sorry, no contest here," the man said. "Wrong number." There was silence on the other end of the phone. Then the man said, "I'm hanging up now. Have a nice day."

"Wait!" Tommy and his parents all shouted at once. Cracker Jacks barked some more.

The voice on the other end said, "I'm just kidding; this is the right number. Can you describe the card?"

"Yeah, I'm holding it right now," Tommy said, trembling slightly. "It's leather."

"And?"

"And it has a bunch of writing on it."

"OK, for official confirmation I'm going to need you to read me the code written on the back left corner of the card, please."

Tommy flipped the card over and read the code: W-43-I-52-LL-543-IZ-5954-DA-591-M-797-AN

"Very good," the man on the phone said. "Now write down only the letters on a piece of paper and leave out all the numbers."

Tommy waved for his parents to get him a piece of paper and a pencil. They scrambled around the kitchen and handed him a pencil and the envelope from a credit card bill. "OK, I'm doing it now," Tommy said. On the envelope, he carefully wrote down the letters and left out the numbers.

W-I-L-L-I-Z-D-A-M-A-N

"I got it."

"Great! Now read it to me."

"Will iz da man," Tommy read, unsure if he was saying it right.

"Again! Nice and loud this time," the man demanded.

"Will iz da man!" Tommy repeated, louder than before.

"One more time, like you mean it!"

"WILL IZ DA MAN!" Tommy shouted.

"You got that right, kid! I like your gumption. Allow me to introduce myself. My name is Will Panzell. I'm the owner of the Riptide, and you are my new left fielder. Welcome to the team!"

"Thanks," Tommy said, his heart racing a million miles an hour. "I'm a huge fan, but I'm only ten years old."

"I know you are, T—" He stopped in midsentence. If Tommy didn't know better, he would have thought the man had almost called him by name. "Pardon me. What I'm trying to say is… What's your name?"

"Tommy."

"And you're only ten?"

"Yeah."

"Oh! Too bad, Tommy. You can't win the giveaway. The cutoff is eleven years old. I'll have to give the card to someone else. We appreciate your interest, though."

Tommy's heart dropped. He'd wanted this opportunity so badly, and the thought of losing it because he wasn't old enough was too much to imagine.

"I'm just kidding! How lame would that be, if you found the card and then couldn't be the left fielder because you're a kid? I don't care if you're ten or ten thousand. You're my new left fielder. Can you play well?"

"I play Little League, but I'm not very good."

"That's fine. You should fit right in. Be at the field Monday morning—and don't forget to wear a cup!"

40

THE KID
CAN'T PLAY

The announcers on ESPN were ranting during the Sunday morning show after they learned about the winner being a child. Tommy watched in amazement. He'd watched ESPN a million times, but never imagined his picture being on the screen or the announcers talking about him.

"Well, folks, if you didn't think Will Panzell was crazy before, you'll probably agree he's nuts now. This guy has just added a ten-year-old to his roster!" one of them said.

"It's unbelievable. Do you know how many guys in the minors would give their right arm to play in the big leagues?" the other added.

"Yeah, I used to be one of them. I can't imagine being a pro player and learning that everything you've ever wished for was just given to a kid."

"I can't imagine the commissioner is going to allow the kid to play. It seems it's just another publicity stunt from the owner of the Riptide."

"I agree. As you know, the commissioner's office hasn't approved of the card giveaway from the beginning. Can you imagine this guy goes through all the trouble of giving away this special card, and he doesn't even get permission from the commissioner's office? Also, Will Panzell seems to have ignored the fact that MLB has a sixteen-year-old age limit. The kid can't play."

41

WELCOME TO
THE CIRCUS

The next morning, Tommy woke up only half-believing he was on a major league team. He brushed his teeth, got dressed, ate breakfast, and then clicked on ESPN to make sure it was real. They kept showing an interview with Will over and over again.

"I have the right to staff my team as I see fit," Will said. "My contract gives me complete control of that, and the commissioner can tell you it's all there in black and white. I don't need his permission to staff my team. If I want to put a bullfrog in a baseball uniform in right field, then guess what? You're going to see a bullfrog play right field for the Riptide."

Tommy's mom and dad took off from work to drive him to the stadium. His heart beat double-time as his dad pulled into the player parking area. He laughed to himself when he saw the line of kids along the chain-link fence waiting for autographs. He was usually one of the only people standing there before games. He was shocked by how many kids were at the stadium. He had never seen it so crowded. Media people, reporters, and camera crews lined up as far as he could see. The kids waved him over, holding their baseballs and pens. Tommy reluctantly walked over.

"You're the kid that won the raffle. You're the luckiest kid in the world," one kid said.

"I guess I am."

"Sign my ball," the kid said, like it was the most obvious thing ever.

When he was bored at school or doing homework, Tommy had practiced signing his autograph countless times on the backs of his notebooks and folders. Signing the ball felt natural, like he was meant to do it.

He signed the kid's ball and the line of people grew even longer. They all wanted Tommy to sign their ball, hat, shirt, whatever. His dad videotaped the scene and his mom held her hand over her mouth in disbelief.

T-Bone had just parked his car. He walked over and said, "Hey, kid. Welcome to the circus."

42

YOU'RE SO MONEY

Tommy signed a few last-minute autographs and then he walked into the stadium. Shawn welcomed him immediately.

"Hello, Tommy; welcome to the Riptide. I just need your dear old dad and mum to sign this contract. Congratulations on your win. What can I get for you?"

"Nothing. I'm just psyched to be here," Tommy said as his mom and dad signed the contract.

"We can't believe he won," his dad said. "But what's the plan here? Are you guys going to let him hang out for the day or something?" He handed the contract back to Shawn.

Shawn placed it in a folder, which he tucked under his arm. "Mr. Night, the team lawyer, will explain everything to you. He'll be right over."

Charlie walked up in full shark suit. He took off his shark head. "So this is our lucky winner. Congratulations, young man. Welcome to the team. We're very excited to have you with us."

"We were just asking Shawn what the plan is for tonight," his dad said. "Will he get to sit in the dugout or watch from seats close to the field?"

"Oh, he's a roster player. He'll be playing in the game. Let me take you to your suite. Mr. Panzell will be in shortly to greet you. Morgan St. John will meet you out on the field for batting practice a little while later."

Tommy'ss suite was amazing. It had his name on the wall and everything. Tommy and his parents were completely amazed.

Charlie said, "I see you have a jersey already. In your closet you'll find a new one with your number and name on the back."

Tommy opened the closet and took out the brand-new jersey. It was awesome. His last name was stitched on the back. He was surprised to see that his number was a dollar sign.

"Mr. Night, how come I don't have a number?" he asked politely.

Will walked in and said, "Because you're money, kiddo. I owe a lot of people a lot of money, and I have a feeling you'll help me pay it all back. Without you, there's no season two for the Riptide."

"Hi, I'm Tommy. I'm really happy to be here, sir."

"I know who you are, kid, and you can save the 'sir' stuff for my grandpa. Call me Will."

"Thanks, Will," Tommy said. "I can't believe this is happening. It was the weirdest thing. I got this pack in the mail and—"

"Never mind the details, kiddo. You found the card. It doesn't matter how you found it."

Tommy was so excited he talked a mile a minute. "I'm so happy to be here. You have no idea how big a fan I am. I've been to every home game. I can't play big-league-level baseball, though. I bat .238 in Little League, and that's with a pitching machine."

"Nonsense, son! You've got to believe in yourself. Today you'll be hitting against a major league pitcher. Should you be worried?" Will asked.

"No?" Tommy asked, unsure of his answer.

"Of course you should be worried! You should be absolutely terrified. If he hits you with a pitch, you'll probably crack in half." Will slapped Tommy's dad on the back and winked.

"Maybe he shouldn't go out there," Tommy's mom said apprehensively. "He could easily sit in the dugout and watch."

"No chance, my good woman! The contest clearly said the winner would play left field, and the boy will play left field. You'll be living every kid's dream, Tommy."

Tommy's dad said, "That's incredibly generous, Mr. Panzell, but isn't there a rule forbidding players from playing if they're under sixteen?"

"Well, look who did his homework. I like your style, Dexter. You're right; there is such a rule. However, I plan to ignore it. Isn't that right, Charlie?"

"Won't it create problems for the league and the team?" Tommy's dad asked.

"Tommy's dad, please don't worry over these concerns," Charlie said. "All you need to know is that your boy will be playing left field tonight and helping us to sell out this stadium for the next six weeks." Charlie and Will high-fived.

"It can't be true," Tommy's dad said. "There's got to be a catch. All my friends are telling me there's got to be a catch and he won't really play."

"Do us both a favor," Will said. "Go place a bet with your friends on it. We'll split the winnings, because tonight your boy is playing left field in the big leagues!"

43

OH BOY

Tommy's parents nervously left him in the dugout and went to their seats. Will gave them the best seats in the stadium, right behind home plate. They could see him in the dugout talking with the team during batting practice. The players were all crowded around him and signing autographs. Even players from the other team came over to the dugout to meet him. Tommy couldn't believe how nice everyone was being to him.

Behind the dugout, there was a media frenzy. Reporters and cameramen lined up along the field, all hoping to get the first interview with Tommy. Will told the press Tommy would be available after the game to talk, but not before. Morgan banned all press from the field and positioned security guards on both sides of the dugout.

"Do you think I'm really going to play tonight?" Tommy asked T-Bone, who sat next to him at the end of the bench.

"You're definitely playing, kid," T-Bone said. "I don't know if you've been paying attention to our season, but Will doesn't really care if something makes sense or not. If he wants to do it, it's going to happen. I wouldn't be surprised if you pitched tonight."

"Yeah, you're definitely going to play," T-Bone's oldest son said. "The owner is completely nuts."

"Hey," T-Bone warned. "He pays our bills, so don't knock the guy."

Tommy had two thoughts as he prepared to go out on the field to warm up. One, he was going to die. Two, he couldn't help wondering what it would be like to actually get on base. He imagined himself on the ESPN highlight reel or the plays of the week. He was shaking as he grabbed his mitt and followed the rest of the team onto the field.

It was exactly like he'd dreamed it would be. The crowd was so loud. He tried to focus on the field and not look at the crowd. Don Tapper walked up to him and put a ball in his glove.

"Don't hurt yourself tonight, kid. Take it easy. If the ball is hit to you, do your best. If it's too high up, let it drop. This isn't about winning. We just need to fill the seats to get a second season."

Tommy trotted out to left field. He threw the ball to Don Tapper at center. It got about halfway to Don then rolled the rest of the way, and was almost at a complete stop by the time it reached him. Don threw it back and Tommy held out his glove to catch it, but missed.

The guys in the booth were doing their pregame. Ken was hotter than ever. "I can't believe I'm even calling this game. I'm seriously considering quitting if this continues. This isn't Major League Baseball anymore."

"Speak for yourself. I'm not planning on quitting over it. But I do agree that this is nuts on too many levels for us to cover in one night," Roger stated.

"The question I have is with Will Panzell's defiance of the commissioner's warning at his hearing earlier in the season. He may have just got himself banned from baseball with this stunt," Ken said.

"Apparently, the one thing Will Panzell is good at is hiring smart lawyers, because his contract with Major League Baseball gives him the power to do just about anything he wants in this stadium. The league was so eager to get his money, it didn't realize what it was setting itself up for with him," Jerry said.

Tommy finished his catch and followed Don Tapper back into the dugout. Don got him a drink and told him to have a seat on the bench. The view from the dugout was amazing. The shortstop, Jeff Zee, sat next to him. The guys on the team called Jeff "Dij," which was short for Digital, because he was always playing with electronics.

"I heard you have a blog. What's the address?" Dij asked.

"Baseballhound-dot-com," Tommy said.

"Cool. I'll follow it. What do you write about?" he asked as he played with his smartphone.

"I write about the Riptide mostly."

"I just followed you."

"Cool! That makes five followers. I don't have many. I just do it for fun and to keep in touch with my grandparents."

"Something tells me you'll have a lot more followers after tonight," Dij said, pointing to the big screen in center field. There was a picture of Tommy displayed next to the words, "TONIGHT, RIPTIDE'S BIGGEST FAN TAKES THE FIELD!" Next to his picture were a bunch of facts about him: age, weight, interests—and then it listed his website, baseballhound.com.

"You're probably right," Tommy said. The whole thing didn't feel real to him. It was too intense to be a dream and too unbelievable to be real. He felt like the luckiest kid in the world.

"Take it in, kid," Dij said, videotaping him. "I'll e-mail you this video and you can post it on your blog if you want."

"Hey, that reminds me," Tommy said. "I saw the shortstop tutorial video you posted on YouTube a few months back. It really helped me with my fielding."

"I didn't think anyone ever watched that thing," Dij said.

"I totally saw it."

"That's awesome, kid. You were probably the only one. Hey, good luck tonight."

"I'm pretty sure they're not going to let me play."

"You should probably go have a look at the lineup card, then," Dij said.

Tommy walked over to where the card was posted on the wall. There it was: his name in the ninth batting position, and he was playing left field.

Morgan noticed him looking at the list and called him over. "Congratulations on your win, kid. I was doing an interview earlier today or I would have introduced myself and met your folks."

"Thanks, Mr. St. John. I still can't believe all this. Are you really going to put me in the game?"

"That was the grand prize, wasn't it?"

"Yeah, but they can't really put a kid in a major league game. My dad told me so."

"In a normal world I would say you're right, but this is Mr. Panzell's world. You're playing in the outfield and batting ninth."

44

I'M CHOPPING ONIONS

"**T**his is complete malarkey," Ken said from the broadcast booth, swallowing the last bite of his burrito.

"It's definitely unorthodox," Jerry said. "But then again, what hasn't been unorthodox with this team?"

"They can't seriously put a child out on the field and expect us to have any respect for the game," Ken fumed.

"Well, I guess we're not expected to respect the game, because here comes the Riptide now.

They're taking the field, and sure enough, there is a child suited up and looking like he's prepared to play," Roger said.

"This is just unbelievable. The kid could get really hurt out there. What are his parents thinking?" Ken asked.

"Well, Ken, our own man in the field, Jay Neel, is sitting with the boy's parents right now. Let's ask them."

Jay Neel sat between Tommy's parents. He held out the microphone to Tommy's mom.

"Thanks for agreeing to talk with us," he said. "I've interviewed many parents of major leaguers over the years. I've even sat with them as they watched their son take the field for the first time in a major league park, but never has the player been a child. Can you share with us what you're feeling?"

"I'm feeling *very* nervous," Tommy's mom said. "It doesn't seem real."

"It certainly doesn't." Jeff turned to Tommy's dad. "How about you, sir? What are you feeling as your son takes a major league field?"

"I'm nervous, but I'm also really happy for him. He's living every child's baseball fantasy, right? He's a kid getting the chance to play in a major league game."

Down on the field, Tommy stood in left field. His legs shook. He looked at all the people in the crowd, the lights, the players, and couldn't believe it was real. He'd always dreamed of being a baseball player and there he was—in the outfield of the Riptide stadium. He slowly turned, taking it all in. The stadium was completely sold out. The crowd whistled and buzzed with noise and excitement. The thunder of the cheers and shouts came together in one surging hum. It felt too good to be true.

In his office, Will stood at the window, eyes glued to the field. For the first time since losing all his money, he looked out over the team and knew the team would make it. The place was jammed. People were eating food; buying jerseys, hats, banners, snacks, and drinks; and there was a kid playing left field.

He got an e-mail from the head of the stadium store letting him know they had already sold out of Riptide jerseys, foam fingers, and hats. For the first time in his life, Will knew his father would be proud of him. A tear formed in the corner of his eye and slowly ran down his cheek.

"Mr. P, the commissioner is on the phone and wants to talk with you," Shawn said through the intercom.

"Tell him I went fishing and I'll call him back," Will sniffled.

"Are you crying, Mr. Panzell?"

"No, Shawn, I'm chopping onions! The stinging onion juice got in my eyes."

"Why are you chopping onions, sir?"

"Mind your own business, Shawn, and tell the commissioner to do the same."

"I think you might want to talk with him. He's pretty upset."

"You know what? Tell him I'm here, but I'm not taking his calls. I'm busy saving my team."

45

THE TEN-YEAR OLD STARTER

Tommy was amazed at the volume of the crowd. It was louder than ever. He had gone to a Yankee playoff game with his dad once, and it hadn't been as loud as this. Will had the crowd enhancer cranked up to ten.

On the field, the ump yelled, "Play ball!"; up in the booth, Ken complained about the integrity of the game; from his office, Will stood at his window, sobbing; and way out in left field, shaking like a leaf, stood Tommy with both his fingers and his toes crossed, hoping the ball wasn't hit his way.

In the dugout, Morgan paced and chewed sunflower seeds. The team had been tough to manage all season and he'd gone along for the ride—but now he was managing a kid? He found it difficult to concentrate on the game because he was so worried about the kid getting hurt.

Owl got set to pitch. Tommy's body rattled from his teeth to his toenails. He watched Owl go into his windup and deliver the pitch. It was a grounder to the left side. The third baseman, Mossey, made the play and threw out the runner.

The second batter struck out. The third batter hit a pop-up to the right side and T-Bone made the catch. Tommy ran back to the dugout. The crowd was still cheering; they hadn't let up a bit since the game started.

Tommy ran down the dugout steps and sat down. Guys drank Gatorade in paper cups and threw them on the ground. Tommy made his way to the Gatorade jug and poured some. He swigged it, crushed his cup, and threw it on the ground. *This is awesome*, he thought.

Morgan waved for him to come over. "Listen to me loud and clear, son: I do not want you to go out there and get yourself hurt. You don't even have to swing the bat if you don't want to."

"Can I swing?"

"Of course you *can* swing. This is a baseball game, after all. It's just that this guy pitching is a major leaguer. He throws, like, a hundred miles an hour."

"That's Wayne Noff. He's lucky if he can hit ninety," Tommy said.

Morgan smiled and patted Tommy on the back. "I didn't realize you were such a fan of the game. What else do you know about these guys?"

Tommy explained everything he knew about Wayne Noff and the rest of the Reds. When he finished, he realized he'd stopped shaking and felt really relaxed and comfortable.

Morgan handed him a bag of sunflower seeds and said, "You're going to fit in pretty well around here, kid. I think you might know more about baseball than the rest of the guys on the team. Sit down on this end by me. Maybe you'll teach me a thing or two."

Jorge George said, "Give me a break, Morgan. He's just a kid. You're acting like he's some kind of expert." Jorge was the least happy to see Tommy, having been the left fielder until Tommy found the card.

"I'll bet he knows more than you about the other team," Morgan said.

"What do you want to bet?" Jorge asked.

"How about a hundred bucks?" Morgan said.

"You're on."

"OK, kid, tell me the name of the catcher on the other team."

"Ryan Hain."

"Correct. Jorge George, what is the name of the pitcher?"

"Who cares?" he said. "Pitchers are all the same."

"Wrong! Kid, same question."

"I'm not looking for trouble, Mr. St. John."

"Answer the question, kid. I bet a hundred bucks on you."

"Noff."

"Jorge, what's his ERA?"

"4.25."

"Wrong again. Kid, same question."

"2.17."

"Correct."

Jorge George was annoyed that a kid was in the dugout showing him up.

"Jorge, what's the pitcher's number?"

"His number?"

"That's what I said."

"Thirty-five."

"Nope. Kid?"

"Twenty-six."

"His hometown?"

Jorge threw his mitt across the dugout. "I give up. He won't know that one, though."

"Kid?"

"Oneonta, New York," Tommy said, feeling bad that he was getting Jorge so mad.

"I'll expect my hundred after the game," Morgan said. Jorge walked off in the other direction.

"Like I said," Morgan said, "you stay by me."

"Yes, sir," Tommy said.

46

BATTER UP!

In the third inning, Tommy stepped into the batter's box for the first time. He tapped the bat on the plate like he had done a million times in Little League.

The umpire said, "Are you ready for this, kid?" The crowd surged. People were on their feet from the front row to the top of the bleachers.

"I guess," he said.

The ump pointed to the pitcher and shouted, "Play ball!"

The pitcher went into his windup and threw a fastball by Tommy that looked like a meteor racing from space into the catcher's mitt. "Strike one," the umpire said. The crowd stayed on their feet. Every kid in the place was jealous of Tommy, and he couldn't wait to get out of the situation. It's frightening enough staring down a ninety-mile-an-hour fastball when you're a grown-up. For a ten-year-old, it was just plain crazy.

He stepped back in for pitch number two. It sailed right by again for strike two. For the third pitch, Tommy held his bat down really low and when the ball came, he simply poked at it. It made contact with the bat and rolled slowly foul. Tommy's hands felt like he had just wound up and slammed the bat against a fire hydrant. His fingertips hurt. He had one more strike to go. The crowd was going bonkers. The pitch sailed by for strike three.

He had done it. He had faced a big-league pitcher and lived to tell about it. The crowd was on its feet. Tommy raised his hands as if he'd just hit a home run in the bottom of the ninth.

"What has happened to baseball?" Ken complained up in the booth. "This is sweet and all, but this isn't a movie, guys. This is Major League Baseball, for crying out loud."

Tommy struck out at his two other at bats. He swung at every pitch, but didn't connect on anything.

By some miracle, there was only one ball hit to left field while Tommy was out. A ground ball that rolled past the shortstop, it was hit softly enough that Tommy fielded it and threw it back. The crowd cheered as if he'd made a leaping catch.

The Riptide lost by nine runs, but no one seemed to care. In the locker room after the game, reporters swarmed around Tommy's locker.

"What was it like to be on a big-league field?" one reporter asked.

"You're living every kid's dream. Explain what it's like," another said.

The reporters stood at his locker for what seemed like a lifetime. After answering all their questions, Tommy headed out to the car with his parents. It was after eleven. His mom complained in the car about how late it was, and how he couldn't possibly keep this up for the rest of the season. Tommy sat in the backseat, smiling. He was in the big leagues.

47

HOW GOOD HE USED TO BE

Afew days later the Riptide were on the field in Arizona for batting practice and the players were all griping about how hot it was.

"How can you guys complain?" Tommy asked. "Don't you realize you're living every kid's dream?"

"Every kid's dream is to work in the hot sun?" T-Bone said sarcastically.

"No, being a pro baseball player. Didn't you dream about it when you were a kid?"

"Maybe when we were kids, kid, but now we're living the reality. Dreams aren't always so dreamy after they come true," T-Bone said.

"What about when you were in your prime? You led the league in home runs two years in a row. What happened?"

"You need to learn to mind your own business, kid," T-Bone said, and walked back to the dugout.

"What did I say?" Tommy asked Jorge George.

"Doesn't really matter much, does it? Some guys don't like being poked like that."

"I was just trying to remind him of how good he used to be."

"I think that's the problem: how good he *used to be.* Maybe you shouldn't. This may seem like some dream come true for you, but for the rest of the guys here, this is pretty much the last stop. We're washed up. We're done. This is the end of the line."

48

YOU'RE A STAR

The team traveled through the night to get to St. Louis for a game the next day. Tommy couldn't sleep. He spent the night on the computer. He kept thinking about what T-Bone and Jorge had said.

When the sun started to come up, he moved and sat in the empty seat next to Morgan. Morgan was reading the paper.

"What's up, kiddo? How are you enjoying your prize?" he asked, smiling.

"It's the best. I still can't believe I'm here."

"Believe it. This is a big part of what it's like. You travel from place to place month after month. You have to either really enjoy it, or really need the money. Have you ever been to St. Louis?"

"No, I've never been out of New York. I can't wait."

"You've got a great attitude. I didn't think you'd make it more than a game or two away from your folks. You're really a fan of the game. I appreciate that. I'm a fan, too."

"I miss my mom and dad, but I'm glad my grandparents are following the team. They're the best. My grandpa is driving right behind the bus right now. They'll stay with me in the hotels. Mr. St. John, how come these guys are losing so many games? Most of them used to be really good players."

"Time breaks a man down over the years. These guys were all great at one point, and that's why I have them here. I thought that maybe there was a little more lightning in the bottle for these guys. But now I think I might have been way off. You can't win if you've lost your passion. All the talent in the world can't replace determination and hard work."

"I think most of these guys still have it. They've just given up a little," Tommy said.

"Some of them have given up a lot. It's a sad thing when a person doesn't use the talent he's got. I gave them their chance. It's a shame they didn't take advantage of the opportunity."

Tommy's mind was busy with thoughts of how he might be able to reach some of the players and help them play better again. "Can I show something to the team before the game today?" he asked Morgan.

"Yeah, what do I care? You can do whatever you want. You're our star, kid."

49

BAD IDEA

A few hours before the game, Morgan finished his pregame speech, announced the lineup, and wished the team good luck. Then he said, "The kid has something he wants to show you guys. So listen up and be nice to him."

"This isn't show-and-tell, Morgan," a voice said.

"I just want to share something with you guys," Tommy said. "I know being on a team with a ten-year-old kid who batted two thirty-eight in Little

League wasn't what you had planned when you joined the Riptide. I want to thank you guys for making me feel like one of the team."

"We're happy you're here, kid," Owl said. "Without you, the stadium would be empty. You just keep doing those interviews, smiling, and filling the seats, and we'll have a second season."

"I know I can't help much in the field or batting, but I think I can help in another way."

"Let's get to it, kid," Morgan said. "These guys need to get out on the field and so do you."

Tommy opened his computer and Dij connected a video projector to it. He turned out the lights. Tommy clicked the play button and the projector showed video of T-Bone when he was a rookie. There were clips of T-Bone cranking home runs and making diving stops at first base. Then it shifted to Jorge George playing in the Caribbean leagues. There were clips of him sliding, diving, and being carried off the field by his teammates when he hit a walk-off in the Caribbean World Series. Then the clips changed to another player, and another, and kept on going for about ten minutes.

When it was over, Tommy turned the lights back on and Dij shut off the projector. There was the sound of someone sniffling.

"Who's crying in here?" T-Bone asked.

"I am," Goggles said. "I'm getting so old. Where did the time go?"

"You're not getting old," Tommy said. "You're still here, aren't you?"

"I'm here, but my ability to play like I used to is gone. I've lost the magic."

"This was a bad idea, kid," Owl said, getting up and heading out to the field.

One by one, the rest of the players got up and walked out, too.

50

USED TO BE

On the bus ride back a few days later, Tommy sat with Morgan. He slept a lot. When he woke, T-Bone was sitting next to him.

"What were you trying to do with that video the other day? Were you making fun of us?" he asked.

"I was trying to show you guys how awesome you used to be."

"Used to be," T-Bone said. "That's what I feel like: a used-to-be."

"So why don't you try to get back in shape? You're still a young guy."

"I don't know where to begin, little man. You'll see when you're older. One day you're doing everything right, and then, in an instant, you're not."

"I know that if you get into shape, you'll play like you did in your prime."

"You ever try to lose a hundred and fifty pounds?"

"No, I only weigh about seventy pounds, so that would be impossible for me. But I bet you can do it. I've seen those shows where people lose tons of weight. They just have to work really hard to do it."

"I haven't worked really hard at anything in a long time."

"Maybe you should start. Imagine how excited your kids will be to see you play like you did five years ago."

T-Bone didn't say anything. He put his earphones in his ears and put a towel over his head.

If Tommy didn't know any better, he would have thought T-Bone was crying.

51

THE TALK

The team bus rolled into the stadium parking lot at 10:00 a.m. Will was out front waiting for them. He waved and danced around as the bus drove toward the stadium entrance. He was in his shark suit.

The guys got off the bus all cranky and tired. The weather was hot and they just wanted to take showers, have something to eat, and get on the field to practice for their four o'clock game against the Mets.

"Can I talk with you in your office?" Morgan asked Will.

Will sat at his desk and offered Morgan a coffee. Morgan stirred the sugar into it and said, "I think the kid is good for the team."

"No kidding he's good. He's packing this place out every night and I'm actually making some money. The way we're going, there will be a second season next year."

"No, not just that. He's having some kind of effect on the guys. He looks up to them and reminds them of when they used to be good."

"I didn't know they used to be good."

"Very funny. I'm not kidding around. The kid was talking to T-Bone for a while on the bus. I've been trying to get that guy on a diet since he got here. After talking to the kid for about ten minutes, he told me he wanted to get a trainer so he can get back in shape."

"Great. He's been eating about a dozen hot dogs a day. Him going on a diet—that alone might save me enough money to survive this season. His kids, too. They eat SO MUCH!"

"Let's focus on the kid. I'm telling you, he's like a little baseball encyclopedia. He knows where each player has played, for how long, statistics. It's pretty amazing. And you know what? I think the guys like him."

"Well, they should enjoy him while he lasts, because next year when I get a real team, I can't have a ten-year-old around."

"Will, you can't talk like that about the team. They look to you for leadership."

"Don't get me wrong. I'll help these guys out next season. They can sell hot dogs, beer, whatever they want. But this team is going to look completely different once I get my checkbook back!"

52

STATISTICATIONER

In the weeks that followed, T-Bone stopped eating as many steaks and hot dogs, got a trainer, and lost a good amount of weight. He was getting in pretty decent shape. The team played a series against San Diego where he hit a home run in three straight games. The Riptide won two of the three. It was the first winning series they'd had all season.

Tommy was a huge attraction. People couldn't seem to get enough of the kid that played left field. It didn't matter to them that he hadn't gotten a hit the entire time he'd been playing, or that he'd had a few balls hit to him but didn't catch any of them. People liked seeing a kid living his dream.

No one enjoyed it more than Will. During one home game, he even put Tommy in as the pitcher after letting fans vote on the Internet for the position they'd like to see him play. His mom was a complete basket case the entire game. The other team crushed the ball. He allowed nine home runs in one inning, walked ten, and got only two outs.

When he came out of the game, Will said, "Great job, kid."

"How can you say that?"

"Because I mean it. That was awesome!"

"How do you not even care that I just gave up nine home runs?"

"That half of the inning lasted almost forty minutes. Do you know how many hot dogs and snacks were sold while you were pitching batting practice to those guys?"

"You don't care if we win or lose. You just want people to come and spend money?"

"It's not just spending the money, kid. I want people to come here and have fun. If watching you pitch to major league players makes them smile and laugh, then that's what I'll give them."

"Doesn't that make us entertainers and not ballplayers?"

"You're living a dream. When people watch you play, they get to share in that dream."

"I just wish I could help my own dream. I'd love to see these guys start playing better. I know they'll continue to get better. I know I'm helping sell tickets and stuff, but we can't win enough games with me on the team."

"You're a lot like me, kid. You like the game for the right reasons and you're a very good statisticationer."

"A what?"

"You're good with statistics."

"That's a statistician. No offense, but how did you make it out of college, Mr. Panzell?"

"Whoever said I did?" Will said with a smirk.

53

OPERATION POWER TUNNEL

The next series was a home series against the Diamondbacks. Will called Tommy to his office before the game started for a pep talk.

Tommy went down to the field and practiced throwing with Don Tapper. He was getting better at catching and throwing. Only about two weeks were left in the season, and he was kind of relieved to finish and get back to real life.

Will held a meeting with Charlie Night, Shawn, and Ron in his office.

"I spoke with Montgomery today and we are very close to being able to pay him back. It's going to be right down to the wire. Charlie doesn't think we can count on ticket and stadium sales alone to make the money back. We need something amazing to drive sales through the roof and make sure we pay Montgomery back every penny."

"What's the plan?" Shawn asked.

"Operation Power Tunnel?" Ron asked with the seriousness of an FBI agent.

Will nodded. "Operation Power Tunnel indeed," he affirmed.

"What is Operation Power Tunnel?" Shawn asked.

"It is one of my most secret weapons in the stadium. No one knows about it but me, Charlie, and Ron. We're telling you because you have to help us pull it off. If you breathe a word of it to Morgan or anyone else, we'll feed you to the sharks," Will warned.

"That's a little harsh," Charlie pointed out.

"You're right. I'm sorry, Shawn. I'm just a little excited, is all. No one is going to feed you to sharks. Just don't tell anyone."

"I won't," Shawn promised, and Will explained Operation Power Tunnel and Shawn's role in it.

54

IT'S GONE!

Morgan was surprised that Shawn was in the dugout during the game. He seemed to be watching Morgan's every move.

"Do you need something, Shawn?" he finally asked in the second inning.

"No, sir. Mr. Panzell just thought it would be a good idea for me to spend the last few home games in the dugout so I can start planning for next year. Are there any improvements you'd like us to make to the dugout over the winter?"

"No. The dugout is too nice as it is. If anything, you should make it less comfortable."

"Great information, Mr. St. John. Make it less comfortable. Excellent idea."

"Shawn…" Morgan said.

"Yes, sir."

"I'd like you to leave me alone now. I have a game to manage and you're kind of driving me nuts."

"Fair enough," Shawn said, but he stayed in the dugout and watched Morgan like a hawk.

While Shawn kept Morgan busy, Charlie, Ron, and Will put Operation Power Tunnel into effect. Ron drove out to the barn he'd driven Morgan through on the first day of the season. He turned on the windmills in the fields around the barn. The windmills generated power to turn the fans mounted on the ceiling of the tunnel. The fans whipped up enough wind in the tunnel that Ron had to be careful not to get caught in it and be blown down the tunnel.

At the end of the tunnel, the gigantic fan Morgan saw on his first day at the stadium started to turn. Charlie clicked a button that opened the wall in front of the fan. It was the back wall of Will's private suite. The suite was about twenty feet higher than home plate. The wind generated from the tunnel could be forced out the front of Will's suite, creating a powerful stream of wind directly above home plate. They shut down the fans when other players were at bat, but when Tommy came up, they cranked them up to full power. If Tommy managed to get the ball twenty feet in the air, the force of the wind would send it sailing four or five hundred feet.

Tommy tried not to think too much about what Will had said and just did his best to make contact. Will may not have cared about winning, but Tommy really wanted to contribute to the team. He struck out on his first two at bats. He was used to it. On his third at bat, the Diamondbacks brought in their worst reliever to face Tommy. He pitched in the low eighties and high seventies and threw the ball right down the middle. Tommy knew that if he was going to get a big-league hit, it would be against this guy.

The guys in the booth called the at bat. "Well, we're probably looking at another out for the kid. You would think it would be mathematically impossible for anyone to get out every single at bat, but he's managed to do it," Roger said.

"If he's got a chance at a hit this season, it's against this pitcher," Ken added.

"Well, let's see if the kid can change his luck at the plate. The first pitch is on its way…He misses for a first strike. I'm kind of getting used to seeing the kid out there. It's amazing he's still in one piece after playing weeks in the majors. The next pitch is on its way. Ball one. The kid showed good restraint on that pitch. If I were Morgan St. John, I'd tell him to take all the way and hope for a walk. Why he's up there swinging the bat is beyond me. The pitcher sets up, and here comes the third pitch of the at bat. It's a ball. Two balls and one strike to the kid. The pitcher resets, the pitch is on the way—he makes contact. It's a weak pop fly to the pitcher, shouldn't be trouble. Wait a second—the ball is sailing for the outfield now. It's going back, way back. It's on its way to dead center field. That ball is now a soaring fly ball and it's deep, it's very deep—it's gone! I can't believe my eyes. The kid just parked one over the dead center field fence. He's still in the batter's box. He looks like he's in shock," Ken said.

"Run, kid," the home plate umpire said.

"What?" Tommy said.

"Run! You just hit a home run."

The crowd went completely berserk. Tommy's family jumped up and down. He looked around the stadium and made eye contact with Morgan, who made the home run signal and shrugged his shoulders. Tommy dropped the bat and trotted to first base.

"Shawn! Where is Will?" Morgan demanded.

Shawn disappeared up the stairs and headed back toward the offices. Morgan knew Will was behind the home run somehow, but couldn't figure out what he'd done.

Once the ball sailed over the fence, Ron shut down the fans, Charlie closed the back wall of Will's suite, and Will looked out on his creation and smiled. Then he made a phone call.

"Montgomery, it's Will. I should be able to pay you back in full tomorrow. I think I'm about to sell a lot of jerseys!"

55

PEOPLE WILL THINK YOU'RE NUTS

After the game, Tommy talked with the media, did a bunch of on-field interviews, and made his way back to the dugout. Will was waiting for him.

"You are some kind of magic, kid. We sold about five million jerseys in the last two hours. I think we're going to have a second season."

"I don't know what happened out there. I just popped the ball up."

"Nonsense, kid. You destroyed that ball."

"No, it was a pop-up. I don't know what happened. I can't even hit the ball over second base. There's no way I hit it four hundred and fifty feet."

"You smashed that ball," Will said, winking.

"You did something out there to help me. I know you want to keep putting me out there to sell tickets, but I think it's time you put a pro back in my position. I'm not helping the team win."

"It doesn't matter. Honestly, this season is coming to a close. I'll only have these guys for a little while longer. Next season I plan on sending them packing and signing some real talent."

"I think you should make some trades and really work on building a farm system. You're also going to have to spend some of that money if you hope to get real talent. I don't think you should trade away everyone, though, because some of these guys are going to turn it around. T-Bone is getting hot and—"

Will interrupted. "You have a lot of ideas about how to build this team."

"I do. I've been a fan from the very beginning. I love the Riptide."

"I know you do. You've been writing about the team on your blog since the day it was announced. You were our very first fan."

"How do you know about my blog?"

"Because I follow it. I was the third person to follow."

"I thought my grandparents and my parents were the only ones who followed it."

"Nope. It was reading your blog that made me decide to pick you."

"You didn't pick me; I found the card."

"Right, but where did you get the pack?"

"I never figured that out. It came in the mail. I always thought my grandparents sent it. Was it you?"

"Yup."

"I'm confused. I thought the card giveaway was for anyone to win. You're saying you had the pack with the leather card sent to me?"

"Yup!"

"But that's not fair. It means no one else had a chance."

"No one else had a chance, but it was still fair."

"Your contest said the leather card was in a pack of baseball cards and whoever found it would play for the team. People were buying packs like crazy hoping to find that card."

"I know."

"But they never had a chance because you had the card the whole time?"

"Yup," Will winked.

"That's not fair."

"Sure it is. I never said I didn't have the card. I just said the person who found it would play for the team. You found the card."

"Yeah, but you picked me."

"Right. Do you think I was going to let just anyone play for my team? You were the most loyal fan I had. I wanted it to be you."

Tommy was confused. He was happy Will had chosen him, but he still kind of felt like Will had cheated.

"Isn't that cheating?"

"That, young man, is called having an edge," Will said.

"I kind of feel like it's cheating. It wasn't fair to everyone else."

"Everyone else wasn't a dedicated fan before I even announced the players on the team. You had faith in me and I wanted to reward you for that. In fact, playing for the team is only the beginning. I have an even bigger surprise for you."

"You're giving me the team!" Tommy said.

"No! No! But now that you have that idea in your head, what I'm going to say might not sound so amazing."

"Don't be silly. What is it?"

"I was hoping you'd be my general manager. To succeed in this game, a team needs a child's spirit to really appreciate it and see things the right way. What better way to capture that spirit than to have an actual child making my trades, signing players, and running the team?"

"What about you?"

"I'm not going anywhere. I'll be here, but I have a hunch you know more about baseball than I do. Let's face it. I almost got myself banned from the league this year. In fact, I may get banned before the season ends after your homerun."

"I thought you didn't do anything to help my homerun?" Tommy asked sarcastically.

"No comment," Will said, smiling. "What about it? How about you hang up your cleats and go out on top. You're already the youngest player to play in the big leagues. You might as well become the youngest general manager too."

"I'd love to, but what about school?"

"It's called a tutor. I had one growing up who homeschooled me, and look how great I turned out!"

"Funny," Tommy said. "People are going to think you're nuts, you know."

"Oh, I'm not worried about people thinking I'm nuts. Every genius has been called crazy at some point in his life."

"So has every crazy person. That doesn't make them all geniuses."

"I like your spunk, kid. That's the stuff I'm going to need from you as my GM. Call 'em like you see 'em. If you think I'm nuts, tell me you think I'm nuts."

"I haven't made up my mind yet. But I definitely want to be your general manager. I'll be here next season."

56

POWER SHIFT

Tommy went back to school the day after the season ended. He rode the bus for the first time that school year. He hadn't seen the kids from the bus all summer and wondered if they still were going to make fun of the Riptide.

When the bus doors opened, Morgan was sitting in the driver's seat.

"All aboard," he said.

"What are you doing?" Tommy asked.

"I'm driving a bus. Me and the boys wanted to make sure you didn't have any trouble on your first day back."

Tommy walked up the steps. Way in the back, seated on either side of Chris and Antonio, were T-Bone and Owl Perz.

Chris waved and said, "Hey, Tommy," like they were the best of friends.

"Don't talk to him," T-Bone instructed. "I don't want you even looking in his direction."

"What are you guys doing?" Tommy asked.

"We're here to support you," T-Bone said.

"Like you supported us," Owl said.

"Hey, it's pretty awesome that you won that contest this summer," the mean kid in the middle of the bus said.

"Yeah, the Riptide is pretty awesome," Antonio added, turning toward the players and smiling an uncomfortable smile.

"Aren't these the guys that said we were losers last spring?" T-Bone asked Tommy.

"No!" Chris insisted. "We were just kidding. You guys are awesome."

Tommy smiled at the guys. "Yeah, they said you guys were awesome."

"That's what I thought," T-Bone said, crossing his arms. "That's what I thought."

Later on, after school, Tommy talked with Will in the dugout.

"How did they get permission to ride my bus?" Tommy asked.

"I gave the bus driver season tickets to let them go for the ride. They got on a few stops before you and had a talk with some of the kids on the bus."

"What did they say?"

"Nothing, really. Let's just say I think your difficulties with those guys are overed."

"Mr. Panzell, you just used that word incorrectly. You do that all the time. How come?"

"I'm not sure. It's kind of confutilizing to most people."

"You do it on purpose, don't you?"

"I most certaintisiously do nots."

"Why? I don't get it."

"This is between us. I don't want to give away all my tricks. It makes people think I'm not the brightest bulb in the bunch. You have to do it at just the perfect moment. Right when people are taking a conversation very seriously and getting really intense. You should try it. It's fun."

"I'll have to considerations that for the future."

"That's my boy. It's called having an edge. You always want to have an edge, my boy."

www.raymondbean.com

Raymond Bean books

Baseball: A Ticket to the Bigs

<u>Sweet Farts Series</u>
Sweet Farts #1
Sweet Farts #2 Rippin' It Old School
Sweet Farts #3 Blown Away

<u>School Is A Nightmare Series</u>
School Is A Nightmare #1
First Week, Worst Week
School Is A Nightmare #2 The Field Trip
School Is A Nightmare #3 Shocktober
School Is A Nightmare #4
Yuck Mouth and the Thanksgiving Miracle
School Is A Nightmare – Quadzilla
(Books 1-4) Special Edition
School Is A Nightmare #5
Winter Breakdown (Coming Fall 2013)
School Is A Nightmare #6 Cupid's Crush
(Coming Winter 2014)

Made in the USA
Middletown, DE
16 December 2015